ALIEN'S TEMPTATION

A SCI-FI ORC ROMANCE

CARA WYLDE

Alien's Temptation

Outlaw Planet Mates

First Digital Edition July 2022

Copyright © Cara Wylde 2022

Cover by Kasmit Covers

Edited by Laura Keysor

THE WORLD OF OUTLAW PLANET MATES

Reazus Prime is a hard planet. Once a prison, it was abandoned when the mines dried up and the Overlords could no longer turn a profit off the prisoners. Now it's a haven for outlaws, pirates, and anyone holding a grudge against authority.

It's isolated, alone, and the only ships coming are the worst sort. One such ship carrying a cargo of abducted human women explodes in orbit. A lucky few were ejected in pods, only to crash on the outlaw planet.

Now the race is on to find and claim the human females.

ANGIE

I t happened the night I went to see the pyramids. The sun had set, but there was plenty of light coming from the city behind me and the three beautiful pyramids before me. As I sat on the rocky slope, snuggled in my hoodie, more to make myself inconspicuous than anything, a ray of intense, white light rained from above and fell right on top of my head.

I looked up, and it blinded me.

The next thing I knew, I was being lifted off the ground.

And my reaction to being pulled up in the air, while I was unable to move or make a sound, wasn't very useful but made sense. I fainted.

I was in and out of consciousness. I could hear voices around me, but I couldn't understand what they were saying. Then I felt a jab in my skull, and another one in my neck. The more I struggled to stay awake, the more exhausted I felt. Until I couldn't fight anymore, and I fainted again, or simply fell asleep.

What had I done to deserve this? I had been kidnapped. That much I figured out. Cairo was supposed to be safe enough for tourists, and I had taken all precautions. All I wanted was to admire the pyramids from a distance, see them one last time before I moved on to the next country on my list.

Maybe my parents were right. And my sister, and my uncle... and all my friends who'd told me not to do it. They'd begged me to not quit my job with the bank, and not spend all my savings on a trip around the world. They'd begged me to stay put. Get a hold of myself, go to therapy if I needed to, and not throw away a good job and a stable future just because I was going through a bit of a crisis.

I hadn't listened to them. I needed a break, so I took it. I quit my job, packed my bags, and booked a flight to Italy. Venice was the first place on my list that I absolutely wanted to see. I visited Rome, too, then Paris, of course, and quite a bit of Spain. When I was done with Europe, Egypt was a must, and then I thought I'd be ready to fly even farther and spend a few weeks in Bali – the Island of the Gods.

What had I done to deserve this? All I wanted was to take a long vacation and find a way to reconnect with myself. Just for a few months, maybe a year, at most. And then, when I returned to the US, I hoped to return with a clear idea about what my purpose actually was. All I wanted was to discover and then rediscover myself.

What I got, instead, was... kidnapped.

If this was the end of me, was I okay with it? As if it mattered anymore... The things I'd achieved and the things I'd failed at...

They must've injected me with something strong, because the slumber I fell into was almost indistinguishable from death. Or from what I thought death felt like.

I opened my eyes, and my vision was blurry for a good minute. I blinked and tried to move, but the space I was in was so cramped that I couldn't even lift my hand to touch my face. I saw white all around me, and a little transparent window through which I could see the sky. My first thought was, "Coffin!" But even for a coffin, the box was too small. Maybe it wasn't made for people like me – short, curvy women in their thirties, with boobs so big that they could barely hold their back straight, and hips so large that buying clothes in physical stores was an adventure with a sad ending.

A coffin, for sure. But as I looked around me, turning my head and craning my neck to try and see better, it looked quite modern. In fact, it looked like it was an advanced piece of technology. And then I remembered the bright light, the shadows of short, thin people, and their voices. And now this... Could it be that I'd been... not just kidnapped, but... abducted? By aliens?

I snorted at how ridiculous that sounded. Clearly, it was taking my brain a while to fully come back online.

I had to get out of here, though. I pressed my palms to the metallic surface and started to push. It didn't budge. I grunted, then let out a scream of frustration, and pushed again. Nothing. Just as I was about to give up, I felt the coffin-like box move. It swayed from side to side, and I heard the squeak of metal rubbing on metal. And then, before I could guess what was going on, the box slid to one side and crashed to the ground. The metal door cracked just a tiny bit, and then I saw a shadow lean over and pull at it until it came off.

I blinked, suddenly blinded by the sun. The shadow moved closer, blocking the light, and I could finally open my eyes and see whom it belonged to. Well, it turned out the shadow belonged to a man. No. An alien.

He was tall, bulky, and his skin was dark green. I stared at him, and he stared at me. We were both in shock. Except my shock was mixed with fear, and his shock was mixed with anger. Or annoyance.

"Wh-what..." I croaked out. My throat was dry, and I found that speaking hurt.

"You're human," he said gravely. "A human on Reazus Prime. How?"

My eyes widened, and this time, I managed to let out a well-rounded "what". Because... what in the hell?! How could I understand what he was saying?! For sure, he wasn't speaking English.

He offered me his hand, and I took it. He seemed to be harmless enough. After all, he'd just opened the damn coffin when I couldn't budge the lid, or the door, or whatever it was. He helped me to my feet, and I was so wobbly that I instantly collapsed. I looked at the white box and finally understood what it was – a pod. Then I looked around me and saw that my pod had landed right on top of a huge spaceship. Yes, a spaceship. I'd seen enough science fiction movies to recognize one.

So, that was why the green-skinned alien was angry. My pod had crashed right on top of his ship, and I could see it had caused some damage.

I looked up at him, and saw that he was still staring at me, maybe wondering if he should help me up again, or if, perhaps, I wasn't capable of walking at all, and he was just wasting his time.

He looked human enough, in the sense that he had two legs, two arms, and one head. The color of his skin gave away the fact that he wasn't human. And he was covered in tattoos! Or, at least, I thought that was what they were... Tribal drawings that covered his chest, back, and arms. They weren't black, as tats usually were, but of a coppery red that complimented his dark green skin quite well, I had to admit.

He was ripped, too. Hard, taut muscles everywhere, and I didn't mind it one bit that he wasn't wearing a shirt.

Now, his green skin didn't bother me that much. His tusks, though... Yes, tusks. Sharp and long, poking out of his mouth and curling over his upper lip. His eyes were dark, and his hair was raven black. But the tusks... I found it hard to look away from the tusks!

"Human," he said again. "How did you get here?"

"I... I don't know." I looked at the pod, at his ship, then at our surroundings. We seemed to be on a beach. Then I looked up at the sky, and finally understood why the light burned so bright and hot. There were two suns! "Where am I?"

I removed my hoodie and was both surprised and relieved when I realized by backpack was still attached to my body. Because I was wearing it in the front when they'd abducted me, the aliens had probably thought nothing of it. Maybe they'd thought I was even bigger than I actually was. They hadn't removed my hoodie and hadn't inspected me. Did that mean they were in a hurry?

He cocked an eyebrow. "You're on P79 Rigus System, also known as Reazus Prime."

"I... I don't know what any of those words mean." I sucked my lower lip in and munched on it. It was cracked. I was so thirsty that I could barely think.

"Here," he said, and handed me a strange bottle.

I took it, opened it, and sniffed the liquid inside.

"It's water. Drink."

"Thank you."

I drank greedily and watched him as he turned away from me. He cursed under his breath, and the words weren't translated perfectly in my brain, because I understood maybe half of them. I scratched the back of my head, and I felt there was some pain there. I remembered the jab, and it hit me that my kidnappers had probably installed a translation device into my brain. Otherwise, how was I able to understand everything the orc man said?

Yes! An orc! That was what he was. What other creature had tusks like his? And also green skin...

"You're an orc," I said.

He ignored me, busy with his tools as he tried to fix the damage my pod had done.

I stepped closer to him.

"You're an orc, aren't you?"

"What?"

"Orc," I said again. Was he deaf or something?

Exasperated, he turned toward me and shot me an annoyed glance.

"What are you on about, human? I don't know what that word means, and the translator doesn't know, either."

"You don't know what an orc is? It's like... a fantasy creature... umm... monster. Yes! A fantasy monster with green or gray skin, and with tusks, just like yours."

He blinked, then shook his head and returned to his work.

"I'm not a fantasy creature, much less a monster. Or an orc. I am Zokunian."

"What's a Zokunian?" I drank more water and leaned against the side of his ship.

He let out a growl and looked at me like he wanted to murder me, so I jumped aside and put distance between myself and his spaceship.

"You've done enough damage for one day, human. I don't have time for this. I don't have time for you, and I'm only trying to fix the ship so it can fly to the Hub. It will need more fixing after, if I want to make it back to Zorran. But until then, I'm on a mission, and I'm behind already. So, step aside, be done with your babbling, and let me work."

"Hmph." I crossed my arms over my chest. "I only asked a question. What's a Zokunian? And what's Zorran? And what's the Hub? Also, my name is Angie. Stop calling me human. It doesn't sound very flattering."

"Angie."

He stopped for a moment and looked at me. Our eyes met, and he held my gaze for well over a minute. It felt like we were suspended in time. A dozen thoughts went through my mind. Was he trying to decide what to do with me? So far, he'd been nice. He'd helped me out of the pod, and he'd given me water to drink. But my presence clearly annoyed him. I'd crashed on top of his ship at a very inopportune moment. He was on a mission, he'd said. And I was in his way.

"Angie." His brows furrowed when he said my name a second time. "Zorran is the name of my planet. Zokunian is my race. And the Hub is the place where you might find a solution to your predicament. Angie, you have to know that the planet you landed on, Reazus Prime, is very dangerous. It's not a good place for someone like you."

"Someone like me?"

"A human female. A universal breeder. You were lucky that you crashed on top of me."

On top of him. I grinned before I could stop myself.

"And why's that?"

"Because when I fulfill my mission and return to Zorran, I will become a priest. I will take no mate, and I will pledge myself to the Three Heads."

Okay, he was losing me. I was more confused than before.

"Even though you've slowed me down, Angie, I will help you again. I will take you to the Hub, where you can catch a ship back to your planet, Terra. But first, I have something to do on this island."

"Island?" I looked around me again.

"You will wait for me here."

"Here... where?"

"Inside the ship. You'll be safe." He threw his tools into a box. "I have to go now."

"No, wait!" He was ignoring me once more. "Wait! You can't leave me here!" He was strapping weapons to his belt, daggers and firearms, and getting ready to leave me behind. "Wait!" I started rummaging through my backpack. Tissues, lipstick, my wallet, tampons... finally, my phone! Of course, there was no signal. "What's your name? At least tell me your name!" I threw the backpack over one shoulder and started running after him.

"It's Thev'rar. You can't come with me, Angie. This is one of the most dangerous islands on this planet. Sorahan Island. It's better if you just wait for me on the ship."

"No! No, no, no..." I blocked his path, and he ran right into me. My hands came in contact with his very bare, very strong, very ripped chest. His skin was warm, and I could feel the beat of his heart. "Please, Thev."

"Thev'rar."

"Thev, please... I have no idea what's going on."

"It's clear to me. Humans don't know about the existence of other species in the universe. You are not evolved enough to be entrusted with such knowledge.

Sometimes, however, slavers ignore that, and they abduct fertile females to sell them on other planets. You were abducted, kept on a slave ship, and something happened, and the ship crashed. I saw it myself, a ship splitting in two in the sky. I just didn't know what it meant then. I will take you to the Hub and help you get back home. But not now, Angie. Now you have to move out of my way."

"Slave ship..." My eyes filled with tears. Finally, my mind was starting to wrap itself around what had happened to me, and I was flooded by overwhelming emotions and a painful realization – I was, indeed, lucky that Thev had found me and that he was a nice person. A nice orc. "Please don't leave me..."

He jumped back, and confusion mixed with unease flickered in his eyes.

"What are you doing?" he said. "Stop that."

"Stop whaaaat?" I cried harder, because I was certain he was going to leave me, and I couldn't deal with the idea of being alone on an alien planet. I didn't care his ship was safe. I couldn't be alone.

"Th-that..." He motioned at my face.

"I can't!" So, my tears were making him feel uncomfortable. "Please, take me with you... I won't be a burden, I promise."

"Fine! You can come with me! Now stop... doing... whatever you're doing."

I sniffed and wiped my tears with my sleeve, then dug inside my backpack for tissues.

"What am I doing?"

"Spilling water out of your eyes."

I blew my nose and stared at him, wondering if out of the two of us, he might've been the crazy one.

"Crying? I'm not spilling water out of my eyes. I'm crying. Don't tell me your... umm... species doesn't cry."

He narrowed his eyes at me. "No, Zokunians don't cry. And why would we? It looked like you were having a miserable time."

"You're right. I am having a miserable time!" I carefully placed the used tissue in a pocket I used for the trash. Being on an alien planet didn't mean it was okay to throw litter. Then I smiled up at Thev. "But I'm feeling better now. Where are we going?"

He sighed, shook his head, and carefully moved around me, so as not to touch me, as he resumed his brisk walk toward what looked like a deep, dark forest.

"Fine. Don't tell me."

THEV

The last thing I needed was to have the fate and safety of a universal breeder – a human – in my hands. She wasn't only confused, clueless, and clumsy. She was also a danger to me and my mission. If the slavers who'd abducted her were alive, they would be looking for her and all the other females who'd escaped. But the slavers weren't the only problem. The second the outlaws on Reazus Prime figured out the crashed spaceship had just rained a bounty of innocent, luscious human females on their planet, the hunt would begin. They would want them for themselves, or they would want to capture and sell them for profit. Either way, Angie, as she called herself, wasn't looking at a bright future.

Unless she made it to the Hub unscathed and she managed to catch a ride to Terra. But then she'd have to pay for the ride, and I doubted she was in possession of any credits.

Did I care enough about her well-being to sponsor her?

I looked at her over my shoulder. She didn't notice my stare, as she kept her head down and focused on putting one foot in front of the other. I could tell she wasn't used to this kind of effort. She was struggling to keep up with me, and I slowed down a little. I was in a hurry, and I didn't want to waste any more daylight, but the pathetic way in which she was sighing and grunting made me feel bad. She often stopped, closed her eyes, and put a hand on her chest, as if to try and calm down her erratic heartbeat. It didn't help that she was carrying a bulging bag on her back.

She was innocent and luscious, indeed. All human females were, to some extent; at least that was what I'd heard from others. This was the first time I was seeing one with my own eyes. She had soft hair, the color of the first sun on Reazus Prime, and flushed lips the color of the second, smaller sun. Her skin was smooth and perfect, slightly tanned. Her eyes were big and blue, and now that I thought about them, I shuddered as I remembered water spilling out of them. Crying, she'd named it. I didn't want to see her do that again, though I couldn't quite say why.

Her body was short and voluptuous. When she'd faced me, earlier, her tiny hand on my wide chest, her head had barely reached my sternum. Her shortness and obvious frailty were endearing, I had to admit. Though, again, I couldn't quite say why I felt that way about her. Maybe it was because she was new and interesting. The first human female who'd touched me and whom I had touched, if only for a brief moment. Yes, that had to be it. Nothing more.

I wasn't fascinated with her curves, no. Only to the extent to which the roundness of her hips and the heaviness of her breasts confirmed she was a universal breeder, one of the best in the universe. Anyone in my position would've probably snatched her at the first chance he got, and safely tucked her inside his spaceship. Not me. I was to be a priest, and priests on Zorran didn't take mates. Had I met Angie years ago, I would've considered it. But now I was too old. The fact that I hadn't met my soulmate in my twenties, when all Zokunians who were fated to build families took mates, only meant that I was not to have that fate.

I was meant to pledge myself to the Three Heads – the triple deity the Kingdom of Zo'kun worshiped. I felt that was my destiny, and I was here, on Reazus Prime, the worst outlaw planet in the universe, to make sure I could fulfill it.

I was here to find my sister and bring her home, where she would become queen. Only then, knowing that the kingdom was in her good, fair hands, I could retreat to the temple and spend the rest of my life in prayer.

"Oh God," I heard her mutter under her breath. "Dear God, what have I done to deserve this?"

I assumed the name she kept repeating was that of her deity. I often invoked the Three Heads when I found myself in challenging situations.

I stopped and waited for her.

She almost bumped into me. She winced, looked up, and apologized.

"This is a nightmare! And where is the light?" She motioned at the dark forest. We'd managed to enter it, but we were far from our destination. "It's damp, and it stinks. What are these trees?"

"I'm afraid I don't know what they're called. I'm not an expert in off-world botany."

"Will it get even darker?" She squinted at the rare slivers of light that managed to penetrate the thick canopy. "And this mud..." She lifted one foot to inspect the squishy ground. "Where are we going, again? What is your mission?"

I sighed and resumed walking. She was asking too many questions.

"Oh, come on!" I heard her follow me. "Let's at least make some small talk, okay? It will help make time go faster. This trek is killing me! I mean, thank God I'm wearing the right shoes and all, but still... I wasn't mentally prepared for it."

"I told you to wait on the ship. Had you listened to me, you would've been comfortable now. And I wouldn't have to slow down every five minutes."

She picked up the pace, marched to my side, and poked me in the arm. I looked at her, confused. She grinned at me, then pouted. That took me aback. Her human face seemed to be capable of ranges of emotions I had never seen in the females of my species. It was hard for me to read her.

"Come on! Where are we going? What are we doing here?"

I once again put some distance between us. When she was so close, she made me feel things I didn't understand.

"I am here to find my sister. You, on the other hand, are here because you're stubborn."

"You're right, I'm stubborn. Especially when a green-skinned alien with tusks wants to leave me behind on a mysterious island. And that, after he tells me the island is dangerous."

"It's more dangerous out here than on the beach. You should've listened to me."

"So, your sister... She's on the island?"

"I believe so. I landed at the Hub last night and asked around. Not everyone I talked to told the same story, but more than a few mentioned Sorahan Island. If Ta'sha is here, I'll find her."

"And then what?"

"Bring her home."

"Oh, so she ran away?"

By the Three Heads, she was asking so many questions! But she was right. Talking did make time pass faster. We were deep in the forest now, and the terrain was becoming treacherous. Even I had to slow down and make sure I stepped where it was safe.

"She didn't run away. When our mother, the queen, died, our father fell into a deep grief. Ta'sha's relationship with the king suffered. He was harder on her than on me, and Ta'sha has always been a free, wild soul. He was probably afraid he would lose her, too, but unfortunately, he showed his love for his daughter in all the wrong ways. Ta'sha decided to leave Zorran and travel for a while, discover other planets, species, and cultures. She's always been passionate about off-world art. She's a collector."

"Oh. Your sister sounds amazing. I'd love to meet her."

I cocked an eyebrow. Why would Angie ever want to meet my sister? I let it go.

"But now our father, the king, has passed away. He followed our mother into the realm of the Three Heads, and the Kingdom of Zo'kun needs a leader. A queen."

"Why not a king? You must be next in line, right?"

"I am. But I have long decided to become a priest. I cannot be both, so now I need to find my sister and bring her back, so she can become queen."

"Hm. That sounds awfully complicated but thank you for telling me your story. Now, you said this is a dangerous planet. Why would your sister come here?"

Why, indeed?

A merchant at the Hub had whispered in my ear that Ta'sha had followed a pirate to Sorahan Island. She had made a deal with him, and he'd agreed to show her something on this dark, humid slice of land in the ocean. But I wasn't going to tell Angie that. She'd been through a lot already, and the last thing she needed to hear was talk about pirates.

"We'll find out," I said dismissively.

"Well, your mission doesn't sound too difficult." She gave me a smile. "I'm sure we'll be done with it in no time, and then you can take me to the Hub, and..."

She didn't get to finish her sentence. With a surprised yelp, she slipped and fell face-first in a puddle of mud. More like a pool than a puddle...

My first reaction was to laugh. She was flopping like a sea creature on land, trying to push herself up, only to slip again and sink deeper into the sticky, foul-smelling mud. I laughed so hard that I had to hold a hand over my stomach. She started cursing, and the universal translator couldn't quite keep up with it. Most of the words went untranslated.

"Oh, you're awful! Just help me up! I hate you! How can you laugh at me?! I hate you so much!" She flopped some more, until she managed to turn on her back. "Thev! Theeeeev!"

"Okay, okay..."

She had mud on her face and in her hair. Now that I'd calmed down and could take a good look at her, I had to admit she looked quite pathetic, and I felt bad for her.

"I'm sorry, Angie. I shouldn't have laughed."

I offered her my hand and helped her up. She almost pulled me down with her, that was how slippery the mud was.

"Oh, God…" She sighed. She started wiping her face, but since her hands were covered in mud too, she only made it worse. "This is a nightmare!" She opened her bag and started rummaging through it. Then, she suddenly stopped, stared at me, and dropped the bag. "Oh, God…"

"What's wrong?"

I grabbed the bag off the ground, but she didn't want it. Instead, she started scratching at her arms, then her neck and her face.

"Oh, God… It itches!"

My eyes widened. Underneath the mud that was starting to dry on her skin, I could see her pale face turn red. Her neck and chest, too… She was turning an angry shade of red all over, and water spilled out of her eyes again as she scratched harder and harder.

"Stop it."

"I will cry if I want to cry," she yelled at me.

"No, not that… Stop scratching! You're making it worse."

"Worse? My skin is on fire! What can be worse than this?" And she scratched more violently. "This isn't just mud." She stomped her foot in the pool. "What is it?"

"I don't know." I flung her bag over my shoulder and tried to grab her wrists to make her stop. She was starting to draw blood. "It must be poisonous. I told you the island is dangerous. A lot of things can be poisonous here."

I managed to immobilize her hands, but that only made her cry harder.

"We'll go back to my ship. I have medicine."

"I have medicine in my backpack!"

"I doubt your medicine from Terra is going to help you. Come on. Can you walk?"

"N-nooooo!"

I was sure she could walk; she was just in shock. Her skin was flaming red now, most likely all over her body, though I couldn't see underneath her clothes. The rash must've spread, for sure. I didn't have time to argue with her. I lifted her in my arms, and thankfully, instead of scratching herself violently, she wrapped her arms around my neck and hid her face in my chest. She was shaking all over as she kept crying, and the sound of it made my heart ache.

I'd just met her. All I knew about her was that her name was Angie, and she'd been abducted by slavers. Still, I felt like I was responsible for her, for her safety and well-being.

She was human, and oh-so-fragile. She couldn't take care of herself, at least not here, on Reazus Prime. I shouldn't have laughed at her. That had been cruel. I needed to take her back to my ship and heal her.

So, I started running. She was light in my arms, and it was no effort at all. At some point, she stopped crying. She was too busy holding on to me as I sped through the forest and emerged on the beach.

"Wow! You're strong! And fast."

My ship was just ahead. I started toward it, and to my utter despair, it started raining. Just like that. One moment, the sky was clear, and the next, dark, heavy clouds covered the two suns, and rain poured with a vengeance.

"Oh, that's better," she sighed. She turned her face to the sky, eyes closed. "Not perfect, but better."

Fat drops fell on my back, and I was glad when they didn't seem to pinch or burn. I'd heard that, sometimes, the rains on Reazus Prime could be acid. At least we were lucky this time. Angie seemed to enjoy it.

We reached my ship, and she slipped out of my arms. We hurried inside, and I went to find the ointment that I knew could heal anything. Before I'd left Zorran, I'd visited the high priest of the Three Heads and asked him for the best medicine his healers made. When one was set for an outlaw planet that used to be a prison planet, one had to be prepared. Reazus Prime was known for its unfriendly landscape and even more unfriendly beasts. The outlaws that had turned it into their home weren't even the real threat on this rock.

"Take off your clothes."

She'd started scratching again, but when she heard me, she stopped and stared at me like I was insane.

"Excuse you?! No!"

I sighed. "I can't help you if you don't..."

She took off her shirt and remained in only a piece of black lace that covered her round, heavy breasts. I instantly felt my cock harden.

"Just shut up and give me that." She reached for the ointment.

I let her take it, and I tried to look away as she started rubbing it all over her face, neck, and chest. It was impossible, though... not to look at her. Even with her skin so red and inflamed, she was gorgeous.

"I can't... my back..."

I dipped my fingers in the thick ointment and started spreading it over her back. She sighed, took a moment to relax, and then rubbed the cream on her arms and stomach.

"Oh my God... This is better. Way better."

The redness was starting to fade. I was mesmerized as I ran my palms up and down her back. So soft, so warm... I was impossibly hard now, painfully so, and it was becoming obvious enough that she'd be able to see it if she turned to face me. I should've stopped. Her back was covered in the soothing ointment, and there was really no reason for me to keep rubbing her delicate skin.

"Thank you," she whispered. She collapsed on the floor, letting her head rest against the wall.

I took the ointment from her and sat down, too. I was silent, not knowing what to say or do. I felt things for Angie that I shouldn't have felt. Once I returned to Zorran, I would become a priest. I'd made peace with my fate a long time ago, when I realized I was too old to find a mate.

Could it be that I hadn't found her on my planet at the appropriate age because I was waiting to find her here, on Reazus Prime? Because I was waiting for a human female who didn't even know species other than hers existed?

At least we were done, and I wouldn't have to touch her again. Or so I thought.

"I'm going to put this away."

"Wait." She bit her lip and looked up at me, a pleading look in her eyes.

"Are you still itching?" I looked over her curvy body. She was still wearing her pants and boots, and the strip of lace that covered her luscious breasts.

"Mmm... Maybe?"

I furrowed my brows. "What does that mean? Are you still itching, or not?"

And then I noticed the way she was rubbing her legs together.

I blanched. "Oh."

ANGIE

"Turn around."

The itching was getting worse and worse. Even if I didn't get any mud inside my pants, the rash had spread there, eventually. And I couldn't take it anymore. I had to scratch or rub on the ointment. Fortunately, the thing was like magic. It healed my skin almost instantly. Thev had been right. No human-made medicine could've helped me with this predicament.

"Unless you want to do it..."

I bit my tongue, but it was too late. The words had escaped, and they hung in the air between us, now. I gently raised my gaze to meet his. He stared at me like I was the eighth wonder of the world. Which... I had just seen the pyramids. They were incredible. I was not. Or maybe I was, since I'd just managed to render an orc speechless.

I still called Thev an orc in my head.

He cleared his throat. "I don't... know what you mean..."

But the tent in his leather pants told another story. He knew exactly what I meant. He wanted me. It was so obvious. And, truly, I wanted him. Just looking at him was enough to make me itch even more between my legs. And not because of the rash.

He was one fine specimen. His dark green skin didn't bother me. His tattoos were, honestly, to die for. And his tusks didn't bother me, either. In fact, I'd caught myself wondering a couple of times what it would feel like to lick them.

Maybe the poisonous mud had affected my brain, too. Or maybe I hadn't had a good lay in forever. If ever.

It was crazy... what I was suggesting. But wasn't this whole thing crazy? Good God, I was on an alien planet, on an alien spaceship, staring at a hot-as-hell alien man! It was the wildest dream! Maybe I'd fallen asleep watching the pyramids, and the sun would rise soon, I'd wake up, and regret I hadn't screwed the drop-dead gorgeous male with tusks! Those hard muscles underneath that green skin of his were everything a girl could wish for.

And that cock... I wanted to see it free of those sexy leather pants. Was it as green as the rest of him? What did he taste like?

"You know what I mean," I purred, crawling toward him. "If you want, you can do it."

"Do what?"

Could his eyes grow any wider? I chuckled.

"Rub the ointment..." I placed my hand between my legs. "Right here. Where I need it."

In truth, the entire length of my legs was itching like mad. My inner thighs, too, and my buttocks.

His gaze followed my hand, then he swallowed hard and looked me in the eyes again.

"I can't."

"Why not?"

"I am to become a priest. A priest takes no mate."

"You're not a priest now, are you?"

"No."

"Then you can..."

"I shouldn't."

"Are you a virgin?"

He hesitated for a moment, probably wondering if the translator had gotten the right equivalent in his language. It did, because he furrowed his brows and tilted his chin.

"Of course not. I've had mates. Not a soulmate, but temporary mates. Not since I decided to become a priest, though."

I rubbed my legs together. The situation was becoming dire.

"Oh, come on, Thev..."

"I shouldn't sin."

"Well, it's a special situation." I couldn't believe I had to beg an orc whose cock was obviously as hard as a rock to finger-fuck me! I'd never begged in my life. This was a special situation, indeed. I was a mature woman. I knew what I wanted. His hands. On my pussy. "We might as well... Why call it a sin? Here's an idea: what happens on Sorahan Island, stays on Sorahan Island."

Even if he didn't say anything, I felt his resolution weaken. So, I reached out and took his hand. He didn't pull away. I placed it between my legs, and he didn't pull away then, either.

"Angie..."

I let out a breathy moan. I didn't have to guide his hand, because he was rubbing me through my pants on his own. We couldn't take it slow, though. Unfortunately, we were in this position because I actually needed to do something about that stupid rash. So, I quickly undid my pants and rolled them off my legs, along with my panties.

As it turned out, the rash hadn't actually spread between my legs. Just on my inner thighs. As Thev dipped his fingers into the ointment, I sat back and spread my legs for him. Gently, he started with my ankles, and rubbed the cream there, then up my calves and above the knee. Slowly, he reached my thighs, and I moved onto my knees to give him better access. My buttocks needed attention, too, and he used both his hands to spread the ointment over them. He kneaded my flesh, and I could swear that the more he touched me, the more his cock grew in size.

I reached out and undid his belt. Then, one by one, I took out his daggers and placed them on the floor. He didn't stop me. As I pushed his pants down and revealed the prize I'd been craving, he slipped a finger between my wet folds. I closed my eyes and let out a throaty moan. He moved his finger, spreading my juices, making me wetter, then added another. He pushed my folds apart and found my clit.

"Oh, God…" I snapped my eyes open and finally wrapped a hand around his massive cock and looked at it. "Oh… God…"

It was dark green. Darker than the rest of him. But that was to be expected. What wasn't to be expected… the tattoos! They covered the length – the same coppery color that was tattooed on his arms. I swallowed heavily and traced them with the tips of my fingers. He moaned and pushed a finger inside my pussy, and that snapped me out of my trance. I would've asked how he'd managed to get his cock tattooed and if it had hurt, but my brain was already mush. His finger pumped in and out of me, and then his thumb found my clit once more, and I was so horny, so eager for release, that I couldn't form a single coherent thought.

I spread my legs wider and moved my hand up and down his cock. It was so thick that I used both hands, now, trying to give him a proper handjob. I'd never been great at them, but he seemed to enjoy it. Beads of precum gathered around the head, and I spread them all over and pumped him harder.

I was so close... so close... I stared into his eyes, a small grin playing on my lips. His brows were furrowed, and he was completely focused on pleasuring me with his fingers. I cupped his balls with one hand, while I rubbed right underneath the tip with the other. He grunted and finally locked his eyes on mine.

"Thev... don't stop..."

I saw him swallow hard. I pumped him faster, and he shoved his finger deeper into my pussy. My walls throbbed and sucked him in, eager for something bigger. I wanted him to fill me with his cock, but I didn't want to push things too far, too soon.

He came first. Hot cum shot out of his cock, and when I felt it on my hands, my own orgasm exploded inside my core. I squeezed my thighs around his hand and kept him there while I rode the heights of it and pumped him lazily, milking him to the last drop.

And then, it was over. My mind cleared, and I looked down at the mess we'd made. Well, the mess he'd made. His cum was rich and creamy, and I couldn't help myself. I was curious. I brought my fingers to my mouth and licked them tentatively.

"Angie," he groaned. "Don't do that."

He tasted quite delicious. "Sorry," I grinned.

He got up before I could stop him, pulled his pants up, and disappeared down the corridor. I heard water running in the distance, and I knew he was cleaning himself up. I sighed and got dressed. I hoped what we'd just done wasn't going to ruin the friendship we'd managed to build in these few hours since we'd met. He cared about me. I knew it. Otherwise, he wouldn't have bothered with me.

A while later he returned with canned food. I was surprised at how tasty it was. I hadn't realized I was hungry, but as I took the first bite and almost moaned in delight, I knew I was going to eat more than my share.

Outside, the rain was still pouring viciously.

"We can't go out there again," I said. "Not today."

"No, we can't. We'll spend the night here."

"Oh, thank God! I don't think I can walk another step today."

He smiled. "Come on, I'll show you where you can sleep. And we should've eaten at the table. I don't know why we got stuck sitting on the floor."

He took me to one of the rooms on the ship, and I had to admit it looked really cozy.

"Wait, don't go." I wrapped my hands around his biceps when he made to leave. "Please don't leave me..."

"I'm not leaving you," he smiled. "I'll just put everything away, make sure the ship is secure, and I'll be back."

"You promise?"

"Yes."

"I want to hear you say it, Thev. Promise me you'll come sleep with me. I can't be alone. Not even for a second. Or I'll freak out."

He turned to me and cupped my face with his big, warm hands. "I promise, Angie."

"And promise me you won't leave without me in the morning."

He hesitated at that, but then nodded. "I promise."

THEV

I woke up before dawn. Soon, the two suns of Reazus Prime would rise, and it was better to be on the road when that happened. But I looked at the human female nestled in my arms, and I didn't have it in me to wake her up.

Her skin was back to normal – pale and smooth, the softest thing I'd ever touched. Her short, yellow hair was tousled, strands sticking everywhere in the most adorable way. She was so unlike the females of my species. There were no fair-haired females in my kingdom. Zokunians were all green-skinned and dark-haired. We lived in the deepest, lushest forests of Zorran, and our physical appearance had adapted to our environment.

She opened her eyes, smiled up at me, and sighed softly.

"You're staring."

I smiled back. "Sorry."

"Don't be. What are you thinking about?"

"How different you are."

"In a good way, or a bad way?"

"In the best way possible." I threaded my fingers through her hair. "There are no fair-haired, fair-skinned females in the Kingdom of Zo'kun. I once saw a Zolunian female, and her skin was ice-like, and her hair white. But you're more beautiful than that."

At my words, she perked up, her eyes filled with curiosity.

"What are you on about? What's a Zolunian?"

"I'll tell you all about my planet on the walk to the center of the island."

"So, that's where we're headed?"

"Yes." I got up and started getting dressed.

"What's at the center of the island?"

I wasn't going to tell her. Not yet. More than anything, I wanted to leave her on the ship, where I knew she would be safe. But I couldn't do it. Yesterday, it would've been easy. Today, the hardest thing ever. I needed her by my side. I needed to keep an eye on her at all times and make sure she was safe, that she was fed and in no danger at all. It was better to take her with me. But I wasn't going to tell her where we were going and what we were going to do there, because then... what if she freaked out and decided she didn't want any part in it? It would be a smart decision on her part, but I couldn't stand the idea of not having her with me.

"You'll see. Come on, we'll eat first, and then we'll go."

After our failed attempt at getting to the center of the island yesterday, I felt inspired to stuff her bag with a few cans of food, water, and medicine. She wasn't as tough as I was. While I could go for days without food and water without feeling a dip in my energy, she needed to eat and drink every few hours. Also, if she once again fell in a pool of poisonous mud, it was better to have all the medicine I'd gotten on Zorran with me. She insisted on carrying the bag, even after I repeatedly told her that I could carry it. She was a proud one, my Angie. She wanted to be of use. That, or she felt bad because she knew all the food, water, and medicine was for her.

We braved the dark forest once more. She stuck close to me, and I fought the urge to walk ahead. Yes, I needed to get to the cave, and I had to find my sister. But for some reason, Angie was more important than any of that at the moment. At least until we got to the other side of the forest, I would slow down and make sure she didn't get hurt.

"So, tell me."

"Zorran is the planet I come from. It has three continents and two oceans. Each continent is a kingdom ruled by a king and queen. The Kingdom of Zo'kun is where I was born and lived all my life. We live deep in the forest, surrounded by giant trees, and we've tamed most of the wild beasts. Our soil is fertile, and Zo'kun is the richest and friendlies of the three kingdoms. Then, there's the Kingdom of Zo'lun, which is in the north, and is cold and harsh. Zolunians have adapted, and their skin is like ice, their hair white, and their eyes blue. And there's also the Kingdom of Zo'mun, which is in the south, where our giant sun shines the strongest. They, too, have adapted, and their skin is red, and their hair like fire. The three kingdoms are unique and rich in their own way, but I will personally always believe that my race, the Zokunians, are the ones who've been truly blessed. And my sister will make a great queen. Years from now, everyone will talk about Ta'sha Sturmblut."

"Sturmblut? Is that your name, too?"

"Yes. I am Thev'rar Sturmblut."

She gave me a bright smile. "Well, I'm Angelica Parrish, since we're sharing full names."

"Angelica." The name sounded melodious, and I loved saying it. "I will call you Angelica from now on."

"You really don't have to, Thev."

"And you will call me Thev'rar."

"Yeah, that won't happen. Thev is much easier. It flows better, and frankly, it sounds much cooler."

I shook my head, smiling. It had bothered me yesterday, that she didn't use my full name. Not anymore. She could call me whatever she wanted, and it would sound delicious coming from her lips.

We were close to the edge of the forest. I could see light behind the curtain of trees, and I let out a sigh of relief. Angelica had carefully avoided stepping into even the smallest puddle of mud, so she was happy and in one piece.

"We'll stop here to eat," I said once we emerged from the forest.

She looked up at the rocky mountain. "Good call." She dropped the bag she stubbornly carried on her back and took out the water bottle. "I need to pee first."

I blinked, confused as to why she felt the need to tell me that. And then it hit me. Maybe she was scared to go alone, and she wanted me to come with her. So, when she disappeared back into the forest, I followed her.

"What are you doing? I said I need to pee."

"I thought you wanted me to..."

"No! I won't go far."

I furrowed my brows. "It's still dangerous."

She rolled her eyes. "I'll be fine. Now, go. I have no intention of peeing with you watching."

"I wasn't going to watch," I mumbled as I returned to our camping spot.

I prepared her food and waited for her. Five minutes, ten... I glanced at the tree line and listened closely, hoping I would hear her footsteps. I convinced myself that she was fine.

And then the screaming started. She screamed once, and I was on my feet. She screamed a second time, and I was on my way to find her, running through the trees and bushes, not paying attention where I stepped. I found her in a clearing, facing a wild beast.

The beast stood on six legs, its body was covered in black fur, its beady eyes were filled with calculated rage, and it was snarling at Angie as it paced up and down, sniffing the air and getting ready to attack. I'd never seen such a creature before. It must've been native to the planet, or to the island.

"Shh, I'm here," I whispered.

She whipped her head in my direction. Once again, drops of water ran down her cheeks. "It came out of nowhere," she whispered back.

"Angelica, I need you to listen to me. Slowly back away."

"What?"

"I will distract it, so you can run."

"I'm not leaving you!"

"Do as I say."

She wanted to protest again but thought better of it. She stepped back, but when the animal saw that, it lunged at her. Apparently, it wasn't impressed by my presence there. It wanted her. I pulled out my gun and shot it three, four times. Angie ran like her life depended on it. Because it did.

Then, the beast turned to me. I shot it again and again, until I was out of ammunition. It didn't seem to do anything to hurt it. All it did was to enrage it even more.

It lunged at me, and I barely had time to take a few steps back and pull out my daggers. As it snapped at me, I blocked it with my arm and tried to look for a spot where I could stab it and it would matter. Its skin seemed to be rough and impenetrable. The bullets had barely grazed it, even from such close range. As it tried to bite me and tear me to shreds, we rolled on the grass, and I inspected its neck. There were a few patches of skin that weren't covered in the thick fur that covered the rest of its body, and it occurred to me that the fur was like an armor. All I had to do was stab the animal in the neck.

We fought for a while, the beast kicking me with its many legs and managing to bite a chunk out of my arm. I grunted and growled, tackled it to the ground, and finally drove a dagger through its neck. It let out a long howl, and I twisted the blade and pushed it deeper. It stilled finally, and when it gave its last breath, I rolled off it and onto my back. I stared at the thick canopy, letting the eerie darkness of the woods envelop me.

I closed my eyes just for a moment, and when I opened them, Angie was by my side.

"You were out for twenty minutes! I was worried!"

She was doing something to my wounded arm, and it hurt. I tried to get up.

"No, wait. I'm not done." She had her bag with her, and she was rummaging through a small box. "I used the ointment from yesterday. You packed so much medicine, but I don't know what any of it does. I have my own first aid kit, though it's very small. But it has bandages..."

"Bandages?"

"Yes. And I also have some antibiotics... I don't know if they'll agree with you, since they come from Earth. But it doesn't hurt to try, right? With a little luck, the wound won't get infected."

She started patching me up, and I let her. The beast was dead, and I noticed Angie didn't like looking where its body lay.

"Thank you for saving my life," she whispered. "Again."

I grinned. "My pleasure."

"See? I can help you, too. When I packed the first aid kit, I was sure I was never going to use it. But I wanted to look like a smart traveler."

"You're a traveler?"

"Well, if you must know, I was abducted by aliens in Egypt. It was my last night there, before my flight to Bali."

"I don't know what Egypt is. Or Bali."

"Places on my planet. Exotic places that I really wanted to see."

"I'm sorry you didn't get to see Bali."

She chuckled. "I got more than I bargained for. But that's okay." She was done bandaging my wound, and she helped me sit up. My vision was blurry for a second.

She handed me her water bottle. "Bali doesn't have hot, green-skinned aliens with tusks."

It took me a second to realize she was talking about me. I smiled. "I bet it doesn't have poisonous mud and feral beasts, either."

"Yes, it's much less exciting than Sorahan Island. Can you stand?"

"Yes."

She helped me to my feet. I was feeling much better, but I didn't complain when she grabbed her bag and held me by the arm as we walked out of the forest. As a Zokunian, I healed fast. I wouldn't need the bandage for more than a couple of hours.

"You still need to eat," I said.

She winced. "I'm not hungry anymore. Let's just get as far away from this place as possible."

And so, we started our trek up the mountain.

ANGIE

Okay, it was official. I wasn't the best climber. In fact, I was clumsy, and I had a feeling I didn't have the right equipment, either. Had Thev not been there to help me every time my legs wanted to give up, I would've truly been miserable. But feeling his big, warm hands on my hips or around my waist now and then was worth it.

"Why couldn't we just walk along the beach? Find an easier path across the island?"

"We're not crossing the island, remember? We're going to the center of it."

"Right. You still haven't told me what's there and why your sister is there."

"These mountains are not very high. You can do this, Angelica."

I rolled my eyes. He was trying to evade my question, and I wasn't impressed. I turned around and locked my gaze on him.

"Tell me where we're going exactly and how you know your sister will be there."

He averted his gaze and sighed. He didn't want to tell me. But why? Well, I wasn't going to let him get away with it this time. I crossed my arms over my chest, and planted my feet firmly, indicating that I wasn't going to move another inch if he didn't answer me.

"Fine. But you won't like it."

That made my heart clench a bit. He hadn't started on a positive note.

"I need to know, anyway."

"It would've been much easier if you just waited for me on the ship."

"Just tell me, Thev'rar." I thought that if I said his full name for once, it would make an impact. And it did.

"I landed at the Hub and started asking about my sister. She's well known as a collector of art. I was surprised she'd come to Reazus Prime in search of unique pieces, since this planet was once a prison. Now it's a place where outlaws of the worst kind either find refuge or come to make a living."

I shuddered. I didn't like where this was going.

"I found out that Ta'sha had made a deal with a notorious pirate. He promised her to take her to see his treasure that he had stashed in a cave on Sorahan Island. In exchange for what, I don't know. So, I bought a map of the island." He pulled a piece of parchment out of his back pocket and unfolded it. "I can't be sure it's correct, as it is very old. But it's the only way I can orientate myself on the island." He pointed at a place on the map. "I knew I couldn't land my ship there, so I landed on the beach. On the other side of this mountain, there's a cave. I think my sister is there."

"Wow!" My first thought was that his sister wasn't a very bright one. To make a deal with a pirate?! And go alone with him to a cave where he'd hidden his treasure?! I didn't say it out loud, not wanting to offend Thev. "We could be walking right into a trap!"

"I know." He patted the daggers attached to his oversized belt. "I've come prepared. And I will make sure no harm will come to you."

"I mean, I've seen you wrestle with that wild animal, but... pirates?! Space pirates?!"

I started to tremble, and I felt a knot in my throat. I let out a shaky breath and tried to calm down, but it was no use. It wasn't enough that the island was dangerous, and that we were on a planet of outlaws, we also had to go chasing pirates! And I understood that Thev had to find his sister, not just because she had to become queen, but because she was probably in danger... And here I was, stupidly following him. Maybe I should've stayed on the ship, eaten all his canned food, and slept to my heart's desire.

This time, I hadn't only been stubborn, I had also been stupid. Why did I need to be with him all the time? I'd never considered myself the type of woman who easily got attached to men. I'd had relationships, and in none of them had I felt like I was co-dependent. But somehow, for some reason, from the moment I'd met Thev, I wanted to never be apart from him. Sure, because being alone on an alien island was terrifying, but it didn't feel like that was the only reason.

"Angie... Angelica..." He closed the space between us and placed his hands on my shoulders, then my face. "Look at me. No harm will come to you. I promise."

"We'll find your sister, and you'll have to save her..."

"My sister doesn't need saving. Whatever she got herself into, she can handle it on her own. I'm only here to bring her home before she flies off to another planet, and I lose her again."

I took a deep breath and released it slowly. Finally, I nodded.

"Okay."

"I will take care of you," he whispered.

He leaned in, and when I was certain that his lips were going to touch mine, I closed my eyes and lifted myself on my tiptoes. I felt his mouth, passionate and demanding, and I opened mine to welcome his tongue. The kiss was long, and it set my body on fire. He kissed me like this was the first time and the last. I wrapped my arms around his neck and pulled him in, and his hands came to rest on my waist.

"I will always take care of you, Angie."

I bit my lower lip and smiled. "Okay. That makes me feel better."

I kind of wanted to ask him if he'd changed his mind about becoming a priest once he got his sister out of here, but I refrained. There was something between us, for sure, but that didn't mean we were going to be together forever. Right? And I did tell him that what happened on Sorahan Island stayed on Sorahan Island, so maybe he was still going on that premise. It was too soon, anyway. There hadn't even been twenty-four hours since I'd crashed on top of his ship.

We resumed our hike, and finally we found ourselves on the other side of the mountain. We stopped to eat and drink, and I was glad I could rest for a few minutes before we started down the slope.

From up here, I could see Sorahan Island wasn't big. It was a piece of land in the middle of the ocean, with mountains surrounded by dark woods. I couldn't see the beach, or any beach, for that matter. I was hopeful our adventure would be over soon, and I wouldn't have to hike like this ever again.

We started our climb down. I wanted to rest for a while longer, but Thev insisted that the more I rested, the more difficult it would be to get back up and walk. He was right, of course. Even so, it took me a while to get back into the flow – one foot in front of the other. Fortunately, going down was easier than going up.

The terrain was treacherous, though. I couldn't lose my focus, or I'd lose my footing. I held on to him as much as I could, but that was just slowing him down. I didn't want to be a burden. A hiking staff would've been great just about now. I looked for a stick I could use, but there were no trees around. Just rocks everywhere, and I cursed myself for not thinking about it earlier and grabbing something from the forest.

Anyway, I would just have to do my best.

And I did my best, until I stepped on a rock that I hadn't realized wasn't stable and fell before Thev could reach out and grab my hand. I screamed as I tumbled down the slope. I covered my head with my arms and tried to protect my face. The rocks were sharp and unforgiving. I let out a scream every time I hit a particularly merciless one. Their edges scratched me and tore holes into my clothes.

When I finally hit the bottom, I rolled onto my back and stared at the sky. I seemed to be at a bottom of a ravine. I tried to sit up, but there was pain everywhere in my body. I couldn't identify a single part of my body that didn't hurt.

"Thev," I tried to call out, but I was too weak. At least I still had my backpack with me. I pulled it from under me and winced at the pain the movement caused. "Thev," I sobbed.

I heard footsteps nearby, and my heart fluttered in my chest.

"You found me," I whispered.

I tried again to get up, not wanting to look like I was completely helpless. But the boots that appeared in my line of vision weren't Thev's. The next thing I knew, something hit me over the head, and I fell on my face, unconscious.

THEV

"Angie! Angelica!"

I rushed down the slope, but it was difficult to descend without tumbling down myself. There were shrubs everywhere. I got scratched a dozen times, and a rash soon started spreading over my left arm. I ignored it. My body would heal, and if not, I was going to use what was left of the ointment. It was in her bag. I just had to find her.

"Angie!"

She'd fallen into a ravine. All I could do was pray to the Three Heads that she was fine, and she hadn't broken anything. I ran as fast as I could without breaking something myself.

I thought I heard her at some point. I stopped and looked left and right, listening closely. Nothing. Maybe I'd imagined it. I hurried down.

I got to the bottom of the ravine and was shocked to see she wasn't there. No one was. I looked around, frantic to find any clues as to what had happened. She should've been here. I saw her fall with my own eyes, and even though I couldn't follow her trajectory because of the rocks and shrubs, I could guess where she had landed.

I crouched and touched the ground with my fingertips. Someone had laid there just a few minutes before. I could see the shape of a body in the dust. I stood up and walked around, looking for more clues. And then I saw it... Footsteps. Not hers. These were bigger than hers. Wider.

"Angie..."

Someone had found her. Someone had reached her before I did, and they had kidnapped her. I couldn't see any signs of dragging, so they had probably lifted her and carried her. I hoped to the Three Heads that whoever it was, they hadn't hurt her. Otherwise, I'd be forced to spill blood today.

I adjusted my fire weapon and my daggers on my belt and started tracking the bastards who had dared to lay their hands on my human female. Yes, bastards, because the footsteps said there were two of them. And yes, my human female. I'd found her. I'd touched her, and she'd touched me. No one else was allowed to lay a hand on her, or I'd have to cut it.

Maybe I'd been wrong. It wasn't that I hadn't found my soulmate because I was cursed, or because I didn't deserve such love and blessing. Maybe it was because she had never been on Zorran. My mate had been on Terra all this time, waiting for an alien slave ship to deliver her to this horrible planet and into my arms.

I prayed the Three Heads would forgive me for taking back my promise. I couldn't pledge myself to the god of my people when I'd found my mate. It was my duty to claim her now. To find her once more, save her, and take her with me. I'd told her I would fly her to the Hub, where I'd help her catch a ship to Terra. I couldn't do that anymore.

I climbed out of the ravine and tracked the kidnappers to a stream. There, I found Angie's bag. Her things were scattered all over, some of them floating down the stream. I quickly picked everything up, saving as much as I could. The canned food and the water weren't there, which meant the two kidnappers had taken those with them. The medicine was there, though, so I found the ointment and quickly treated the rash on my arm.

This planet was as unfriendly as it could be. At every step, I got stung or scratched, and I didn't have the time or the disposition to pay attention to what touched my skin.

I briefly looked at the map and realized that following Angie's kidnappers meant going in the opposite direction of where the pirate's cave was. But it was a detour worth taking. Ta'sha would have to wait. I hadn't lied to Angie when I told her that my sister was perfectly capable of taking care of herself. Granted it had been a stupid idea to willingly go with a pirate, Ta'sha could take him out if need be.

Nothing was more important than my Angie right now. So, I turned my back to the direction where I knew the cave was in. Angie needed me. I wasn't going to abandon her when I knew she was praying to her own god to send me to her rescue. I would have to ask her who her god was. What his name was, what her people thought he looked like. And I was going to tell her about the Three Heads – the triple deity whose three names we were not allowed to speak out loud. That was how sacred the Three Heads was.

When I found Angie, when she was in my arms again, happy and protected, I would ask her everything about herself and her world. And I would tell her all she wanted to know about myself and my world. It was time for us to get to know each other better. What happened on Sorahan Island didn't have to stay on Sorahan Island. I was going to take her, and all the memories we'd made here, with me. I was going to take her to Zorran, to the Kingdom of Zo'kun. I was still a prince, and I was going to make her my princess.

ANGIE

I moaned softly and moved my head. It felt heavy, and as soon as I opened my eyes, a sharp pain exploded between my temples. I closed my eyes again, waited, and then opened them when I was ready to accept that the pain wasn't going away, and I'd have to live with it for the time being.

I was tied to a tree. My legs were free, but my torso and my arms were well secured with a thick, rough rope. I checked in with my body as best as I could and concluded I was scratched and bruised all over. From the fall, of course. I remembered it. I'd tumbled down the slope and ended up at the bottom of a ravine. And when I thought Thev was coming for me, it turned out someone else had found me. He, or she, or they had hit me over the head, and that hit must've been the source of my headache. I just hoped I didn't have a concussion.

My backpack was missing.

I heard voices nearby, and I strained my ears to listen. There was a buzzing in my head, and I was worried my universal language translator had been damaged. It wasn't something that had been implanted on the surface of my skin. I was pretty sure it was deep into my brain, and if I had a concussion, then it made sense that it would malfunction. Nonetheless, I needed to try and listen to what the aliens were saying.

Of course they were aliens. Everyone on this godforsaken planet was.

I couldn't understand a word they said. They were too far away, and my head was buzzing and ringing. So, I did the only thing I could think of. I started screaming for Thev.

"Thev! Theeeeev! Thev'rar, I'm here!"

The two aliens rushed to me, and before I could take a breath and scream again, one of them shoved something in my mouth. Then, he tied it tightly, and I could barely swallow my own saliva, let alone make a sound. I looked up at them with extreme hatred in my eyes. I tried to show them hatred, and not fear. In reality, I was terrified and quite certain my end was near.

"Shut up," one of them said. "No one can hear you anyway."

They looked like big, nasty lizards. They were both covered in light blue scales. They had long tails, frills at the neck, and what looked like feathers on their heads.

They turned away from me and started talking. This time, I could understand them.

"A human female. A universal breeder. She's a much bigger prize than what we might find in that cave."

"The pirate has riches."

"We don't know what kind of riches, and now that we have her, it's not worth the risk finding out."

"Our father would be delighted if we brought her to him, but also some of the pirate's treasure."

"No. The risk is too great. What if we lose her on the way?"

"Then let's take her to the ship, leave her there, and come back to look for the cave."

The other one hesitated for a minute. He thought hard, then finally shook his head.

"No. Our father will be plenty satisfied with a human breeder. Let's take her to him, so we can earn his forgiveness and forget this all happened."

"You're right. The sooner he welcomes us back, the better. The cave isn't going anywhere."

"We can try again later, yes."

So, from what I was gathering, the lizard men were brothers, and for some reason, their father had banished them or something. And now they wanted to impress him. It sounded like any family drama back on Earth, except maybe here the stakes were higher. Seeing how stealing and kidnapping were in order to be accepted back into the family...

They had been going where Thev and I were going when they stumbled upon me at the bottom of the ravine. The pirate's cave. Seeing how many people knew about his secret stash, I personally thought the guy had to move it.

"She is valuable. We bring her to him, and he won't only welcome us back. He will give us the respect we deserve."

"Yes, yes." The other lizard man grinned. "And everyone will look up to us."

They nodded and chuckled, then turned to me.

My blood froze. They looked at me like I was a piece of meat. Or an object. They didn't even care that I was hurt.

They quickly untied me and pulled me to my feet. They didn't care when I winced and complained, grunting and moaning in pain. My wrists were tied together, and they used the rope to drag me along as they started walking. I blinked rapidly and tried to focus on putting one foot in front of the other. The headache was getting worse, and every single muscle in my body screamed. I was pretty sure I was bleeding from my left side. The sharp rocks had done a real number on me. My ribs were bruised for sure, but at least nothing was broken. Had any bone in my body been broken, I wouldn't have been able to move.

They pulled me after them, and as they started walking faster, I failed to keep up. The terrain was as bad as it had been since I'd left the beach with Thev, and the fact that my vision was more blurry than clear didn't help. I fell in a heap, and when they pulled at the rope, I started crying and refused to get up.

"Come on, human! We don't have time for this."

"She looks hurt," the other lizard man said.

"If she can walk, she's not hurt. She's just pretending."

But I couldn't walk! Didn't they see that?!

I looked up at them with pleading eyes. I tried to speak around the rag they'd stuffed in my mouth, but it was impossible. All I managed was to grunt and croak. I felt so angry and frustrated.

One of them finally crouched down and removed the rag. I spat, took a few deep breaths, and licked my parched lips.

"Water, please."

I thought he wasn't going to care that I was dying of thirst, but then he motioned at his brother to pass him the water bottle. He held it to my lips, and I drank greedily.

"I'm not alone," I said. "Soon, you'll regret all of this, because he'll come for me, and when he does, I don't know what he'll do to you. But you won't like it."

"You're not alone, you say." The one who'd given me water grinned.

"She was calling for someone when we found her," the other lizard man said.

"Who were you calling to? What's his name?"

I pursed my lips. Maybe it wasn't a good idea to actually tell them about Thev. Who he was... I couldn't tell them he was an orc, because he wasn't one. He was a Zokunian from planet Zorran. Would that information scare the lizard men, or give them an advantage? It was better to not find out. I had no way of knowing if they had ever seen a Zokunian before. But if they had, and they knew what to expect, that would definitely give them an advantage over Thev'rar. I couldn't make myself guilty of helping my captors.

"He is bigger and stronger than you," I said.

"Is he?" he laughed.

"I'm serious. He is fully armed, and he will squish you like bugs. Maybe you should consider releasing me now, and he might have mercy on you."

I hoped that would instill some fear in them, but instead, they exchanged a glance, then threw their feathery heads back and laughed harder. It was either that they didn't believe me, or they were making fun of me. That made me so angry that I hoped to God and the Three Heads Thev kept mentioning that he would show up soon and snap these lizards in two.

Just as I was getting ready to say more, the lizard man stuffed the rag back into my mouth and secured it.

"We don't have time for your games, human. Come on. On your feet."

He pulled at the rope, and it rubbed painfully on my wrists, giving me a burn from hell. I didn't fight them this time. I stood up and tried to focus on walking. My head was pounding, and every step was torture. But I had to pay attention and not fall on my face again. My situation was dire already.

"Please, Thev," I begged silently. *"Please find me. Don't leave me."*

As I walked, following the two lizard men and reaching a kind of flow, I thought back to my family and friends. What had I done so wrong to deserve this? Maybe I shouldn't have fought with them. Instead of quitting my job so suddenly, maybe I should've taken a few days of medical leave and sort my head. But no! I had to be stubborn, like I always was. I had to throw everything out the window – my job, my life, my friends... And I had to go on an adventure that had turned out to be nothing like I'd expected.

Here I was now – kidnapped a second time. Abducted by aliens. And my only hope was another alien. A green-skinned, tattooed guy with tusks.

"Please, please... Thev..."

THEV

It was easy to find them. I stayed hidden and watched as they pulled Angie by a rope they'd wrapped around her delicate wrists. She looked awful, not in the sense that she wasn't just as gorgeous as ever, but in the sense that she'd had a terrible fall, and I could see she was scratched and bruised all over. She wobbled as she walked, struggling to keep up with her captors.

They were Nakkoni. I could tell by the scales covering their bodies, and the feathers on their heads. They were young, though, so I knew it would be easy to take them out. But I had to first make sure that Angie was safe. That she wouldn't get hurt as I attempted to rescue her.

So, I followed them in silence, careful to not make a single noise. They were taking her out of the mountains, though. Soon, they would reach the woods that separated the mountains from the beach, and it would be harder to fight them in the darkness. I had to act now, even as I wasn't sure what the outcome would be. Angie was close to them. Too close for my liking. There was another reason why I needed to hurry. We were already quite far from the cave and from my sister. I'd wasted enough time already.

With a prayer to the Three Heads, I jumped out of my hiding spot and lunged at one of the two Nakkoni. I tackled him to the ground and easily knocked him unconscious. But when I stood up, I saw that the other one had a dagger to Angie's throat. I was afraid that would happen.

"Angie…" I snapped out of it before I got ahead of myself. "She's my prisoner," I said. Of course I wasn't going to tell him she was my mate. He didn't need to know she was that important to me. "I found her first, and she belongs to me."

He tightened his grip on her. "Your slave, then? You wanted to sell her?"

"Yes. She will fetch a good price."

"Then why were you headed to the pirate's cave. Don't think we haven't figured that out."

I shrugged. "To rob the place, obviously. More things to sell."

"I don't believe you, Zokunian."

"You don't have to believe me, Nakkoni, as long as you return to me what is mine." I pointed the gun at the other Nakkoni, who was just regaining consciousness at my feet.

We were at a stalemate. One of them had Angie, and I had his partner. Or brother. They did look alike. By the color of their scales, it was entirely possible that they were related. Good. If they were brothers, or cousins, then it meant they cared about each other, and they weren't going to do anything stupid.

"Thev," Angie whispered.

I shot her a quick glance, hoping she understood that I was only lying to get an advantage over the two Nakkoni. My eyes couldn't linger on her, though, or they would guess I was playing them.

"Is that your name?" the Nakkoni who held her asked.

"My name is Thev'rar Sturmblut." I waited a moment, and when nothing sparked in his eyes, I knew he didn't know who I was. The Nakkoni on Reazus Prime were descendants of the prisoners who'd turned the planet into their home after the Overlords retreated. These two must've spent all their lives here and didn't know much about what was out there. Good.

"And Angie is her name?"

"I don't care what her name is. That's what she calls herself. But she's a slave, and once I sell her, her master will give her another name."

I saw Angie's eyes widen at my words, and I hoped she knew I didn't mean what I said. It was true that was what happened to slaves, human or not, but it was not what was going to happen to her. She was mine, and she was going to live like a princess in my palace. Not like a princess. She would be a real princess.

The Nakkoni spat on the ground. He exchanged a glance with the other one, who was still sprawled on his back, and I could tell his resolution was starting to waver. They were truly young and inexperienced. I wondered what they were doing on Sorahan Island. Right. The pirate's cave. They were after the treasure.

I spread my arms wide and grinned at the Nakkoni, revealing my sharp tusks.

"How about we strike a bargain? She's only a slave, nothing more. How about we go to the pirate's cave together and load up on what he has stashed there? The three of us could carry more than one or two of us could. And then, we'll sell all of it, including the human, and split the credits three ways. Everyone wins. Well, except the human."

But they didn't take me up on the offer immediately, which made me think there was something else there. It wasn't about the credits or about becoming rich. I furrowed my brows and waited, ready to strike if things went south. I didn't like that Angie still had a dagger to her throat.

"Let my brother up," the Nakkoni said.

Brother. So, I'd guessed right.

"Not before you let her go. I need to know that we have a deal."

He hesitated for another moment, then sheathed his dagger and pushed Angie toward me. I grabbed her by the shoulders and pushed her behind me. The Nakkoni on the ground jumped to his feet and joined his brother.

"We have a deal."

"What are you doing?" Angie asked in a whisper.

As the Nakkoni were busy arguing in hushed voices, I turned to her. "They're harmless."

"Why strike a bargain with them?"

"We don't know what we'll find in that cave. If my sister is there, the pirate is there, too. And who knows if he's alone."

She shook her head. "You can't trust them." She looked at her bound wrists, and I could see that she was in pain. "That one had a dagger to my throat. Now he doesn't. You could easily..."

"I have honor, Angie." I discreetly loosened the rope without removing it. If anything went wrong and she had to escape, she could now. "I won't strike them down after I'd just made a deal with them. Their time will come. These are young, naïve Nakkoni. They don't know what they're doing."

"Nakkoni?"

"Yes. What did you think they were?"

She huffed. "I don't know. Lizard men."

I smiled. She had a funny name for every species she met.

"Let's go, Zokunian," one of the lizard men, as she called them, said. "We're losing daylight."

They waited for me to take the lead. I knew they were too scared to risk walking ahead and having their backs to me. It was fine. I wasn't scared of them. I gently nudged Angie, and she sighed and started walking.

"You found my backpack, at least."

"I promise you this will be over soon," I said.

"What are you two talking about?" one of the Nakkoni asked.

I looked back over my shoulder. "I was just telling her to behave, or there'd be consequences. What about you two? What were you talking about back there?"

"That's none of your business, Zokunian."

"Where were you taking my slave? To sell her?"

Angie shook her head, and that confirmed there was more to these Nakkoni than they let on. I had to be careful and not underestimate them.

"Again, none of your business. Let's just find the cave, take what we need, and become rich."

I shrugged and continued walking. I would've picked up the pace, but I could tell Angie was having difficulties. I wanted nothing more than to stop, lay her down, and treat her wounds. I couldn't do that, but I could carry her.

"What are you doing?"

I ignored the Nakkoni and lifted Angie in my arms. She snuggled against my chest and closed her eyes.

"She's too slow."

They grunted in approval, and we started walking faster. Her weight was nothing to me. As long as I knew she was comfortable and she could rest, I could carry her forever. I could carry her to the other side of the galaxy.

"I got you," I whispered.

She smiled and relaxed even more.

"I'm so tired, Thev."

"Sleep. I will take care of everything."

"I don't know how you can carry me so easily. I'm not exactly on the light side."

"What are you talking about?"

"I guess you're big enough... And strong enough..." She yawned.

I wanted to kiss her, but I couldn't. The Nakkoni were trying to listen in to our whispered conversation. I heard them move closer, and I picked up the pace.

Maybe I should've gotten rid of them and not complicated things by taking them with us. But it was true what I'd said to Angie... I had no idea what was waiting for us in that cave, and three were better than one.

She was sleeping peacefully now, and I was grateful. I had her in my arms, she was alive, safe, and in one piece. Everything was going to be okay.

ANGIE

I woke up later, having no idea how long I'd slept. It hadn't been a deep sleep, more like I was in and out, listening to what was happening around me, trying to understand what the Nakkoni were saying. But my head hurt, I was feeling dizzy, and I could barely make sense of their words.

"Angie," Thev whispered in my ear. "We're here."

I opened my eyes and saw that it was dark. Three moons were in the sky, and they offered plenty of light. Thev set me on my feet, and I did my best to stay upright. The pain that shot through my calves was indescribable. We were standing before the large mouth of a cave, and more light poured out of it.

"I thought this was supposed to be a secret place."

"It is, simply because almost no one comes to Sorahan Island."

That didn't make much sense to me. Thev left me there and went to talk to the Nakkoni, who'd already stepped inside and were holding torches. So, that was where the light was coming from.

"We're not the only ones here," one of the lizard men said.

Thev nodded. "Do you want to back down now?"

It was a challenge, and it worked. Both Nakkoni puffed up their chests and declared they were going in. They drew their weapons, and Thev did the same. He turned to me, and I could see he was about to ask me to stay behind. I was having none of that. Plus, looking around me, the landscape didn't seem very friendly. There was an eerie, ominous feeling in the air, and I had no intention to wait for them here.

"She's coming with us," one of the Nakkoni said.

Thev didn't protest, and I was grateful we didn't have to argue about it. He probably thought I wouldn't be safe here on my own, too.

"I was certain the pirate would be in space, with his ship," the other Nakkoni said. "You don't seem surprised, though, Zokunian."

Thev shrugged. "I don't know anything. I just hoped he wouldn't be here. But if he is, and his crew is here, too, it doesn't bother me. I can take all of them."

"You sound confident."

Thev fixed him with a dark, intense gaze, and I found that it even made me shudder. "You know where I come from. But do you know what my people can do?"

The Nakkoni swallowed hard, and I hated to say, but I was with him. It was just a flash, but I hadn't seen this side of Thev before. Maybe I was imagining things. My head was on the verge of exploding, and I wasn't thinking straight.

We went in. The Nakkoni led the way with torches, and Thev and I followed them. I couldn't believe we were all working together. The lizard men had kidnapped me, and they had yet to suffer any consequences. I glanced at Thev's profile and wondered who he actually was and what his people could do. What had he meant by that? Or had he merely tried to scare the Nakkoni? I was in over my head, and I understood so little of what was happening. At least my bindings were loose and just for show. That was how I knew that Thev was still loyal to me.

We walked down a long, dark corridor, until we reached an opening. We stepped through it, and before us, a large cave opened up. Its ceiling was high, it was well-lit by torches, and intricate rock formations decorated its walls. But neither of those things was truly impressive. Not compared to what lay in the middle of the cavern.

Piles upon piles of riches. Precious metals, jewels, vases, coins of all shapes and sizes, and even statues and paintings propped against the walls. It was as if I'd stepped into a fairy tale world. My mind immediately went to the story of Ali Baba and the Forty Thieves.

Except it had been really easy to enter the cave. No one had had to utter any magic words.

And among all those precious things... a woman.

The second Thev saw her, he ran to her. The Nakkoni stared, not understanding what was happening, and I gently stepped away from them. I knew who she was. Thev's sister. She looked like him, too, with green skin, copper-colored tattoos, and tusks poking out of her mouth. She was unconscious, lying on a pile of coins. She didn't seem to be tied up, but I could see a pool of blood growing around her head.

"What is this?" one of the lizard guys said. "Who is she? Another Zokunian?"

"She's my sister," Thev said.

"You deceived us!"

"What does it matter? Load up on whatever you want, and let's get out of here."

The Nakkoni sheathed their weapons and did just that. They started stuffing all they could get their hands on in the huge bags they had brought with them.

Thev was trying to wake his sister up. He called her name and gently patted her cheeks and her forehead. I went to kneel by his side and discreetly got rid of the rope around my wrists.

"I have some essential oils in my backpack. If they're still there..."

He gave me the backpack that he'd carried all this time, and I started rummaging through it. My things were a mess, and some of them were missing. I found the oils, though, and I hoped they helped Ta'sha. It was a shot in the dark, but it was the only idea I had. As I put a few drops on the tips of my fingers and rubbed them on Ta'sha's nostrils, Thev stood up. I heard voices, and at first, I thought the Nakkoni were freaking out or were mad that Thev had lied to them. Ta'sha stirred, and I rubbed some oil on her temples. I should've done the same for myself; maybe it could help with my headache.

There was shouting, and I heard weapons being drawn. I looked up and realized we were surrounded.

Now, if the Zokunians looked interesting with their green skin and tusks, and the Nakkoni looked rather scary with their scales and tails, the aliens that were blocking all the entrances to the cavern looked like something out of my worst nightmares. They were massive, burly, and they had boar heads. Round, gold rings pierced their snouts and ears, and their eyes were dark and menacing.

"Widians," Ta'sha whispered when she saw the look on my face. "They're Widians. Nasty creatures." She winced as she sat up.

"Easy. You took a hit to the head." The blood poured out of a gash on the side of her head. I rummaged for my first aid kit, but she stood up and joined Thev before I could stop her.

"I was waiting for you," the leader of the boar men said as he stepped forward.

He was bigger than the others, and he was dressed in expensive clothes, and covered in shiny armor. He must've been the captain.

"At first, the plan was to kidnap this one," he pointed at Ta'sha with his gun, "And make her tell me where she's hiding her personal art collection. I'm a collector myself, you see." He motioned at the glittering pile that was his treasure. "But then I realized who she was. Ta'sha Sturmblut, heiress to the throne of Zo'kun. I knew someone would eventually come for her. And then, I could ask for a generous price. And, of course, for her art collection, as well."

"The throne of Zo'kun?" one of the Nakkoni said. He exchanged a glance with his brother, and then they both looked at Thev, who was paying them no mind.

"I hope you know your plan will never work," Thev said. He was calm and collected.

"I see you brought a human slave with you. I heard talk about a ship full of them breaking in the atmosphere and crashing on the planet. I was thinking tef going hunting myself, but now I'm glad I didn't let my crew take care of this particular business. So, new proposal – I will have the human, plus whatever riches the Kingdom of Zo'kun can spare, and your sister's art collection. And then, I'll let you take her home. I'll let all of you walk away, even the Nakkoni, who will first have to empty their bags and pockets."

Ta'sha took a step toward the pirate, and Thev had to grab her by the arm to hold her back.

"You're delusional. Just because you knocked me unconscious when I had my back turned, like the coward that you are, you think you have a chance to get what you want? You don't know what you got yourself into, Widian."

"I beg your pardon, princess. I believe you don't know what you got yourself into." He spread his arms wide and motioned at his men. "You are surrounded. We outnumber you. This has been my plan all along. I made everyone believe that I was on my ship, in space, minding my pirating business, when in fact, all my men were here, waiting for me to bring you in. And then we all waited for him to make an appearance." He turned to Thev. "You must be her brother, prince Thev'rar Sturmblut. I am glad you came yourself and didn't send a lowly guard."

"It is my duty to protect my sister."

At that, Ta'sha did something I didn't expect. She sighed and rolled her eyes. Then she smiled at Thev and teased him.

"You really shouldn't have come, big brother. You know I can take care of myself."

"I know. That's not why I came."

She cocked an eyebrow.

"I came because the king is dead, and you have to return home, sister, and become queen."

She stared at him for a moment, mouth agape. She hadn't expected him to say that. I tried to read her expression, but it was hard. Thev had told me that since their mother died, Ta'sha's relationship with their father had deteriorated. And that was why she'd left home to go on adventures and find alien, unique art for her personal collection. Now, I couldn't tell if Ta'sha was sad at hearing about their father's death, or indifferent.

She hung her head, and I had my answer. Even though she and the king had had their differences, she was sad that he'd passed away.

"Did he suffer?"

"No. He went peacefully, in his sleep."

She nodded. "I will come home."

The pirate huffed. "This is a very touching moment, but may I remind you that you're not going anywhere unless you pay me what I'm owed?"

"We don't owe you anything," Ta'sha said, pouring vitriol in her voice.

"Funny." The pirate ignored her and tilted his chin toward me. "Let's start with the human female. Universal breeders are hard to come by, and I must admit I've always dreamed of having my own."

I broke into a cold sweat at his words. The look he gave me made me sick to my stomach. I took a few steps back, until I was positioned between Thev and Ta'sha, and the two Nakkoni. To my surprise, the lizard men stepped forward, and I ended up behind them. If the Zokunians got robbed, then the Nakkoni got robbed too, and that didn't sit well with them. Still, they were four, and I counted at least a dozen of the pirate's men.

This was more than a nightmare. This was hell.

"She is not a slave," Thev said. "She is my mate, and you will not lay a finger on her."

My heart skipped a beat. He'd just called me his mate. What was going on? What did that mean? Not that I didn't like it, but... if he said I was his mate, then I wasn't going to see Earth again anytime soon.

THEV

The Widians did have the upper hand. They were many, and they were heavily armed. I looked over at my sister, and she nodded. She was ready, and so was I. I looked over my shoulder and saw that the Nakkoni were behind me, and Angie was safe. I was surprised they were still here, determined to fight. I would've expected them to give up on the treasure and bargain for their lives. But apparently, they wanted the pirate's riches badly. It could've been for credits, or for something else. Angie knew, but she hadn't had the chance to tell me the Nakkoni's true story. Not that it mattered to me. What was important was that they were here, and if they couldn't make much of a difference in the fight with the Widians, they could at least keep Angie out of harm's way.

Ta'sha and I stepped forward and away from each other. We both needed space for what we were about to do. The pirates advanced, weapons and daggers at the ready. My sister and I didn't bother to reach for our weapons. Not yet.

I took a deep breath, and as I released it, I reached inside myself and searched for the beast that was there. My chest expanded, and with it, my arms and legs grew longer and wider. My whole body grew until it was three times its normal size. Beside me, Ta'sha did the same – reached for her inner beast and allowed it to take over.

I heard gasps of surprise and saw the pirate captain's eyes dilate. Not many knew what Zokunians could do. We turned into beasts when we had to, and even though it took a toll on us, we never lost a battle.

I saw red. When the beast took over, I lost a piece of myself, if only for a few minutes. I was unstoppable and untamable.

Bullets started flying, but neither I, nor Ta'sha cared. They couldn't pierce our skin. The captain threw a dagger at my face, and I easily blocked it with my arm. It clattered to the ground like a toy. I let out a growl and lunged at him. He'd hurt my sister, and he wanted my mate. I couldn't let him live.

None of them could live.

And there was no escape for them, because when the beast was in control, it wanted blood. It didn't stop until the enemy was obliterated.

I threw myself at the captain, and we tumbled to the ground. He tried to fight me, and he was strong and determined, I had to give him that. He pulled out two other daggers and started stabbing me, but the blades barely did any damage.

Meanwhile, Ta'sha was throwing pirates against the walls left and right. She yelled and howled with every victory, and when they got up and attacked her again, she grinned in delight. She was playing with them. She had always been like a big, feral feline when she turned beastly.

Me... I was different. I saw no point in playing with my prey. Just as I was about to snap the captain's neck, two of his men jumped on my back and tried to pull me off him. I stood up, flexed my biceps, howled, and turned to get rid of them in one swift swoop. Blood splattered on the ground and the precious metals and stones nearby. The captain managed to scramble to his feet.

"Stop! Stop this, and we can make a bargain. A fair one."

I furrowed my brows, squeezed my hands into fists, and started walking toward him. He started walking backwards.

His men were still fighting Ta'sha, and I could tell she'd gotten bored of them, because they were starting to fall and not get up. There was blood everywhere.

Farther away, I saw the Nakkoni fight, too. One of them was wounded and on the ground, on his knees, while the other one was shooting at the pirates and trying to protect his brother.

Angie was in a corner, eyes wide and mouth agape. She looked like she was in shock, but what truly mattered to me was that she was safe. The pirates had tried to get to her. Now they all knew she was my mate, and they knew that getting their hands on her was the only way to stop me. Too bad I wasn't going to let them do that.

Ta'sha was done with her attackers, and the Nakkoni managed to kill the pirate that had stabbed his brother. Only the captain remained. And he was mine.

The Widian looked around him, at the horror and bloodshed. He then looked back at me and held up the only dagger he had left.

"Let's talk about this, Prince Thev'rar."

But I wasn't Prince Thev'rar anymore. I was the beast. And the beast did not negotiate.

I lunged at him. He yelled as I knocked the dagger out of his hand, and looked up at me with wide, shocked eyes as I grabbed him by the throat and lifted him up. His legs kicked helplessly, and he tried to pry my hand away as he was choking. I squeezed once, and his neck snapped. His eyes bulged out of his head, and then he gave his last breath. I dropped him in a heap on the stone floor.

It was over. I looked around me, and all our enemies were dead.

I started taking deep breaths, and soon, the beast began to retreat in the depths of my soul. My body returned to normal, and I could finally feel all the places where the pirates had shot me or tried to stab me. My skin was intact, but my muscles had registered the blows. A weakness seeped into my bones as a result of giving the beast control. It had sapped me of energy, and I was this close to collapsing and falling into a deep sleep. But I couldn't afford to do that. I would rest later.

Ta'sha looked just as exhausted. With a sigh, she sat down with her back against a statue of some alien god.

I turned to the Nakkoni. One of them was lying on the ground, and the other was hovering above him, trying to wake him up.

"Brother," he said. "No, no..."

I knew his brother was dead.

I locked eyes with Angie, and she cowered in her corner, pressing herself against the wall and hugging her bag to her chest. I smiled and walked to her.

"I promised you I would keep you safe," I said.

Her eyes widened, and she shook her head. "No. Not like this."

I frowned. "Angie?"

I stepped closer to her, and when I crouched down, she scurried away. I felt a pain in my chest. She was afraid of me. Terrified. I raised my hands to show her that I meant her no harm.

"Angie, it's me. You don't have to run from me."

She got up and did just that. At first, she headed toward Ta'sha but changed her mind. To my surprise, she actually moved closer to the Nakkoni who'd just given up on trying to wake his brother.

"Stay away!" She threw her bag over one shoulder and looked around her. She grabbed the nearest dagger she could find and held it close to her body. "I mean it, Thev'rar. Stay back."

My heart sank. Angie had seen my beast, and now she was lost to me.

ANGIE

I saw them change before my eyes. Thev'rar and Ta'sha. They grew in size, their tusks lengthened and sharpened, and they were so strong that nothing could hurt them. I saw them tear all the alien pirates apart. Blood covered the floor and the walls, and even the treasure that was piled up in the middle of the cavern. It was a bloodbath.

"Hey, little human. Are you okay?" Ta'sha had gotten up, and she was standing right behind me.

I turned around and pointed the dagger at her. My hand was shaking.

"Don't," I whispered.

She raised her hands. "I'm not going to hurt you. Angie, is it? My brother said you're his mate. I would never, ever hurt you, Angie."

"I don't believe you! I don't know you, and I don't trust you! Stay back."

I could feel tears starting to form, and I did my best to keep them at bay. I was scared like I'd never been in my life, and tears would've made me look even weaker. Thev'rar had already seen me cry a few times, and he'd expressed his opinion about my spilling water out of my eyes. Orcs didn't cry, I had to remember.

"Angelica." His voice was gentle and careful.

I stepped to the side, so I could have them both in my line of vision. The Nakkoni had dragged his brother's body away, and he was now busy stuffing more jewelry and coins into his bags. It was back to business, apparently.

"I am so sorry, Angelica," Thev'rar continued. "I can explain what happened. I'm sorry you had to see it... see me and my sister like that. But we had to do it. We were outnumbered. It was the only way."

I shook my head. "I don't know what I saw."

"It's something we Zokunians can do. We each have a beast inside us, and we can release it to win any battle, any fight. We don't do it often. It takes a huge toll on us, and I will have to sleep for days to fully recover. I'm in a great amount of pain right now, even if you can't tell."

I bit the inside of my cheek. He did look like he was in pain, but what did I know? Beast? I didn't want to have anything to do with any beast.

It was just dawning on me now that I had no idea who the green-skinned alien before me was. Thev'rar

Sturmblut. Prince of some faraway kingdom. When I first met him, he wanted to be a priest. Now he claimed I was his mate, and he didn't want to be a priest anymore. His devotion to his god didn't seem to run very deep. What was I to understand from that?

"Angie, please... What can I do to make this better?"

"I don't think there's anything you can do."

I heard Ta'sha starting to rummage through the pirate's treasure, as well. She was looking at vases, statues, and pulling paintings out to see them into the light of the torches. The Nakkoni said something in protest, but she snarled at him, and he backed away. They were interested in different things, anyway, and there was plenty for both of them. She wanted the alien art, and he wanted everything else.

"You are my mate. My fated mate. I know that now."

I glanced back at Thev'rar. I could barely look him in the eyes now, knowing what he'd done just a few minutes before.

"I can't live without you, Angie. I need you by my side."

"I can't..." My voice sounded choked. "I can't be with you."

He ran a hand through his dark hair, his lips pursing and his brows furrowing. That made me take another step back. I was making him mad, but I couldn't do what he said.

"If you would just listen to me, let me explain... Come with me to Zorran. Let me show you my world."

"No! God, no! I can't." The last thing I wanted was to be surrounded by more aliens like him, more aliens who could go berserk. "Thev'rar, you have to let me go."

He paled. The color drained from his face, and for the first time, he was almost as white as I was.

"Don't say that," he murmured.

A tear slipped down my cheek, and I wiped it quickly, before he could see it. I hated that I had to do this. I'd really thought he was someone I could spend more time with. Maybe someone I could spend my life with. He'd protected me like no one had ever done it before. He'd treated me like I was special, and I'd fallen for it. He'd been more gentle and caring than any man I'd ever been with on Earth.

But this side of him... I didn't think I could live with it. Thank God the cavern was large and there was plenty of air to breathe, otherwise I would've fainted from the smell of blood.

"I can't go with you."

He shook his head. "Okay. Then at least let me keep my first promise to you and take you to the Hub. I will buy you a ticket to Terra myself, and you can go back to your life."

That was exactly what I intended to do. Go home. But not with him, not on his ship.

I looked over at the Nakkoni, who sensed my gaze. He cocked an eyebrow in a silent question.

"Will you take me to the Hub?" I asked.

He looked at Thev'rar, then back at me, and shrugged. He didn't know what to say. I wasn't just a slave anymore; I was the orc's mate. He was hesitant to tread on this dangerous ground. He'd seen what he'd done to the Widians, and he surely didn't want to become the next recipient of his vengeance.

"I will help you carry your brother's body in return," I offered. "And the bags, too."

"Angie, don't do this," Thev'rar said. "You can't trust this petty creature."

"And I can trust you?!" I whipped around and fixed him with an intense gaze. "Look around you! Look at what you did! How can I trust you?!"

"Because I would never... ever..."

"Please stop, Thev. And just let me go. Let me go."

"I'll take you to the Hub," the Nakkoni finally said. "If you help me carry my brother's body to my ship."

"You, shut up!"

I saw the rage in Thev's eyes, and I moved closer to the lizard man. When he saw that, he calmed down.

"He will betray you," he insisted. "He will sell you the first chance he gets."

"No, I won't," the Nakkoni said.

At this point, all I knew for sure was that I couldn't trust anyone. Of course I couldn't trust the Nakkoni, but at least he wouldn't turn into a murderous beast if he got mad. What I had seen here, in this cave, had changed me forever. From now on, I was going to do things my way.

"Thev, I'm going, and you can't stop me."

Hoping he wouldn't do anything stupid, I gently slid the dagger into my backpack and went to help the lizard man. He'd filled three huge bags, and they were impossibly heavy. He gave me two of them, and he slung the third over his body. Then, he carefully crouched down and lifted his brother. I had no choice but to struggle with the two bags and follow the Nakkoni out of the cave.

I dragged them more than carried them. The alien was stronger than me, but even so, I could see it wasn't easy for him to carry his brother's body. If I wanted to get off this cursed island on a ship other than Thev's, then I had to do this. I had to carry the heavy bags, push them and pull them as best as I could.

"How far is your spaceship?" I asked. "Do we have to cross the mountains?"

"No. It's the same way we came, then through the forest until we reach the beach."

I was glad the Nakkoni had landed in a better spot than Thev. Sure, it was harder to get to Thev's ship from where we were, which probably meant it was safer, but right now, what mattered was to not die trying to cross those mountains again, and with the insane burden I was carrying.

We walked in silence. I was grateful he set a reasonable pace, also because that told me his species wasn't as strong, and fast, and deadly like Thev's species. Maybe I still had a chance to get out of this alive and with my freedom. I had a weapon now, and seeing how one of the Nakkoni had died from a single well-aimed stab, it could actually be of use in a moment of crisis.

I could do this. I just had to be resilient, fight to survive. I was a big girl. I didn't need anyone to take care of me. Sure, it had been nice to know I didn't have to lift a finger when I was with Thev, and he'd saved me more than once, but that didn't mean I was helpless.

I could do this. I could get back home.

THEV

I had no choice but to respect Angelica's wishes. I watched her go with the Nakkoni, my heart feeling dead in my chest. There was a lump in my throat, and it sent a buzzing pain through my jaw and my head. My eyes started to sting, and for a second, I thought water was going to start dripping out of them, like I'd seen so many times happen to my human mate. It didn't happen to me. Zokunians couldn't cry, not even when their heart was broken into little pieces. I had to push the hurt down, so I could function, but I found that I couldn't do it. Not this time.

When my mother, the queen, died, I suffered and mourned her. The next day, I was by my father's side, helping him run the kingdom. When he died, too, I mourned him for a day and a half, then I went looking for my sister. The future was more important than the past, and the moment Angie had walked out of the cave, she'd become my past. This was the way of the Zokunians. But as I stared at where she'd been, at the spot where she'd huddled in fear, I couldn't accept it. It felt wrong.

"I've got everything I wanted," Ta'sha said. "We can go."

She'd wrapped a bunch of paintings in cloth and stuffed some of the smaller statues and vases in a bag she'd brought with her. She wasn't interested in the rest of the treasure, just the art. It wasn't stealing if she took from a pirate. A dead pirate, at that. It would've been politically correct to find out where the pirate had stolen the art from and give it back. But I knew my sister wasn't going to do that. She was obsessed with her art collection. Once those paintings were added to it, they would never again see the light of day.

"Let's go," I said.

We exited the cave and saw it was still dark. This night was going to be a long one. My thoughts immediately went to Angie. Where was she now? The Nakkoni wouldn't harm her yet, as he needed her to help him carry his load. But once they reached his ship... what then?

"So, the human female," Ta'sha said. "Tell me about her."

"There's not much to tell." We started walking, and I set a punishing pace. The sooner I got off this island, the better. "I met her yesterday. She fell out of the sky, in a stasis pod."

"Come on, brother. Don't be like this. Just tell me."

I shrugged. I knew what she wanted to hear, but I wasn't in the mood to talk about it.

"Back there, you said she's your mate."

"I thought she was, but she's clearly not."

"Well... Maybe you're right. If she can't stand the sight of a true Zokunian warrior fighting, then she can't be your mate."

Her words were like a dozen stabs to my chest. I looked at her profile and wondered when my sister had become so blunt and cruel. When we were little, she was the one to help me up when I fell and scratched my knees, she was the one who stood up for me in the face of bigger, older children. She was my big sister, and she was good and fair. Or used to be. This world had changed her. Or, better said, the worlds she'd seen since she left Zorran.

I didn't say anything. It was better to be silent. We were going to get to my spaceship, then off this rock. Home, she would be crowned queen, and finally, I'd be free to join the priests of the temple of the Three Heads. I hadn't been destined to have a mate, after all. It had been nice to feel hope, and dream otherwise, but it was over now, and it was okay. In time, I'd make peace with it. I would never regret having met Angie. And I'd never regret what we did on my ship on the first night. I swore to myself she was the last female I touched. Whatever happened next, I didn't want to soil her memory.

We started climbing the rocky mountains, and I helped Ta'sha with her load. I couldn't stop looking in the direction where I knew Angie and the Nakkoni were headed. I felt a pull, and I did my best to resist it. Every few minutes, my mind would start to wander, and my feet led me astray, much to my sister's confusion.

"This way, Thev."

Of course I knew the way. It was just that my heart didn't want to follow it.

We reached the other side of the mountain and started climbing down. I remembered how Angie had fallen, and how I couldn't stop it, reaching for her when it was too late. Had she not fallen, the Nakkoni wouldn't have found her and taken her prisoner. Maybe none of this would've happened. But that made no sense, and I had to remember that what ruined any chance I might've had with her was the way I'd behaved in the pirate's cave.

Not for a second had I thought that if she saw my beast, she would be frightened. In my world, Zokunian females were impressed when they saw a male's beast surface. It was proof that he was strong and worthy. Proof that he could take care of a female, so that she wouldn't have to push herself and release her own beast. But Angie wasn't like the females on my planet. She was human, and she was small, kind, and delicate. I didn't know a lot about humans, but I had heard physical strength wasn't one of their attributes. They relied on fire weapons, mostly, which in a place like Reazus Prime, didn't do much good. The Widians had learned that the hard way.

So, of course Angie was frightened when she saw my beast. She wasn't cruel, and it wasn't in her nature to be violent. I should've figured that out before I ruined everything. I should've fought fairly, with weapons and daggers, even if it meant risking my life and my sister's. Even if it meant risking Angie's life. At least, she wouldn't have told me to leave her alone. To let her go.

We reached the edge of the forest, and we stopped for a moment. We were making good time, both eager to leave Sorahan Island behind. We drank some water and looked at the dark trees. The three moons were still in the sky, but they would soon fall over the horizon, and the two suns would rise. By then, we'd hopefully be at the ship.

"Tell me what you're thinking, Thev."

I shook my head. "Let's go. The forest is the worst place on this island, and I want to get to the other side."

"Are you thinking about her?"

"You said it yourself. She can't be my mate."

She sighed. "What do I know? I haven't found my mate, either. The only difference between us is that you took it as a curse and decided to become a priest. Is that still what you're going to do?"

"Yes. Nothing's changed."

"Everything's changed, Thev."

We entered the forest. It was darker and fouler than during the day.

"Look, why don't we get to your ship, take it, and go looking for that Nakkoni's ship. They couldn't have made better time than us. They're carrying a body and three bags of coins and gems."

"She wouldn't want me to do that."

"She was in shock, Thev. I'm willing to bet she didn't know what she wanted. If she refuses you again, fine. But I think it's worth a try."

I laughed bitterly. "Do you think I can take a second refusal, Ta'sha? Do you think my heart can take it?"

She tilted her chin and looked me up and down, her eyes like steel. "You're a Zokunian. A prince and a warrior. You unleashed the beast, and you're still standing. Look at you. You're exhausted, and you haven't fallen yet. By the Three Heads, I'm ready to collapse, but seeing your determination gives me strength. You can take a second refusal, and even a third. And then, you can convince her to come with you, because you're fated to be together."

I ran a hand over my face. I was covered in sweat from the exertion, and I was dirty and bloody from the battle.

"Do you mean that?"

"I mean it. Now, come on. Let's get to your ship, and then let's get your mate and go home."

I grinned, feeling new strength pouring into my limbs. Now, this was the sister that I remembered. Apparently, back there, we'd all been in shock, and we'd all made poor decisions. If I didn't give up now, maybe the damage could be undone.

ANGIE

We were almost out of the dark woods, but I was barely alive. Or at least, that was how I felt. I was drenched in sweat, and I had to stop every five minutes, or I would collapse. The Nakkoni seemed to be just as unhappy as I was. It wasn't easy for him to carry the body of his dead brother, and also a bag full of riches. As for the bags I'd agreed to carry for him, I was dragging them on the ground, pulling at them as if they were two huge boulders.

"You're aliens!" I shouted at him.

"No, you're the alien," he said boredly.

"I would've expected you to have some kind of technology to help carry this stuff!"

"Our father disowned us. All we have is a ship, and it's not in great shape, either. But after I bring him the pirate's treasure, he will welcome me back. That is, if he doesn't blame me for my brother's death."

"Your father sounds like an unpredictable A-hole."

"I don't know what an A-hole is, but unpredictable... yes. You could say that. To thrive on Reazus Prime, one has to be tough. And my father is one of the toughest men I know."

"Thrive? Is that a thing? I'd be happy to survive."

"In your case, yes. You're human. You can't thrive of Reazus Prime. You can only hope you'll be lucky enough to fall in the hands of a master who will treat you well."

I wanted to say something, but I pursed my lips instead, and swallowed my words and my pride. The lizard man had said he'd take me to the Hub if I helped him carry the load to his ship. The last thing I wanted was to anger him. I couldn't quite trust him, as things were. If I also was a nuisance to him, he could change his mind in a second.

When we finally emerged from the forest, the two suns were shining brightly. It had taken us all night to reach the beach, and I was grateful for the light. It felt like I hadn't seen it in ages. I stopped for a moment, closed my eyes, and turned my head toward the sky. I could feel the warmth starting to dry my drenched clothes. I was dreaming of a shower.

"Come on, human."

"My name is Angie."

He ignored me and started toward the ship. It was smaller than Thev's, and it was in a sorry state, indeed. The paint was peeling off. It looked old and worn.

Suddenly, I wasn't sure I wanted to fly in it. It didn't look safe at all.

The Nakkoni dropped the heavy bag and disappeared inside with the body. I dropped the other two bags beside his, placed my hands on my hips, and looked around. There was a sound that hadn't been there before, and it wasn't the sound of the waves crashing against the shore. I looked to the west, shielding my eyes with my arm, and that was when I saw it. Thev'rar's ship.

With wide eyes, I watched it land at a safe distance from the Nakkoni's ship. After a few minutes, Thev jumped out.

The lizard man appeared next to me. I glanced at him and saw the exasperated look on his face.

"I thought I wouldn't have to see the Zokunian again."

I wanted to say the same, but I couldn't. The words stuck in my throat. As Thev'rar approached us, I found that I wanted to run to him. I forced myself to stay put. My heart was hammering in my chest, and I silently cursed it for being so weak and gullible. I tried to remind myself of what I saw in the cave. Thev and his sister had ripped the pirates apart like it was nothing. If Thev seemed big now, in the light of the two suns, I had to remember that he'd grown three times larger when he'd let the beast take over.

"Angie." He stopped a few feet away, seemingly not wanting to get into my personal space and freak me out.

There was a pleading look in his dark eyes. "I'm glad to see that you're well. That you've made it out of the mountains and the forest."

My stomach fluttered at the thought that he'd been worried about me. I should've said something, but I remained silent. It wasn't very polite, but I was afraid that if I opened my mouth, the wrong words would come out. Words that I wouldn't be able to take back. It was better to wait and see what his intentions were.

He took another step toward me.

"Angie, please come with me. Don't go with him." He tilted his head toward the Nakkoni. "You can't trust him."

"And I can trust you?"

"What happened last night... I know I frightened you. I'm sorry. I promise I will never let you see me like that again. That was the first and last time. I will never again unleash the beast in your presence."

That made me feel a little bad... On the one hand, it sounded reassuring, but on the other hand, if the beast was a part of him, it seemed unreasonable to stop him from being himself. But it was a ruthless part of him. Even if I wasn't the recipient of that unbound rage, it was something that was hard to watch. It was hard for me to know that he was capable of it.

I sighed. I looked over at his ship, but I couldn't see Ta'sha. I looked at Thev, and then at the Nakkoni, who was just getting the three bags to carry them onto his ship.

"Tell me, and please be truthful," I addressed the lizard man. "If I go with you, will you sell me as a slave?"

He looked at me and shrugged. "No. But I will take you to my father as a gift and let him decide."

"I really can't trust you…" I was disappointed.

"You should go, if you want to go," he said. "Go with the Zokunian."

"Why would you let me go now, when I'd be such a nice gift for your father?"

"You helped me carry my brother. That, and I've seen what he can do." He threw a quick glance at Thev, then averted his eyes. "I don't want to end up like the Widians. I got what I wanted, and it will have to be good enough. I won't step foot again on Sorahan Island."

Oh God, I was really left with only one option. I had to go with Thev.

I stepped away from the Nakkoni's ship, figuring out he would want to leave as soon as possible. I turned to Thev, shook my head, and closed the distance between us. He wanted to reach out for me but stopped himself. He didn't know if he was allowed to touch me.

There was nothing that I craved more than his touch. I was glad he'd come for me. He was here even if I'd rejected him. He hadn't abandoned me.

"Will you take me to the Hub, like you promised?"

"No."

I furrowed my brows, but that was when he fell onto his knees and scurried closer to me.

"Angie, I don't want to take you to the Hub. I don't want to buy you a ticket back to Terra. I want to take you with me, to Zorran. I want to take you to my kingdom and make you a princess. My princess. I want to show you my home in the deep, green forest. I want to wake up by your side every morning, and I want to count the stars with you at night. Angie, you are my mate. We are fated to be together, and that's why we found each other. I've been looking for you, waiting for you... I thought I'd never find you. I will not become a priest. I want to become your man."

I realized that I was shaking. There was a knot in my throat, and my eyes stung with tears. Once again, I kept them at bay. I didn't want Thev to think he'd just upset me, when in fact, I was happy beyond words.

No one had ever declared his love to me in such a sincere, direct way. No one had ever looked at me like Thev was looking at me right now – like I was the only thing he wanted in this world, the only woman for him. And it felt... amazing. To know that I was desired with such force. To know that this man wanted to take care of me and offer me a life I hadn't even dared to dream.

I nodded, not trusting my voice to speak.

He beamed at me. "Yes? Is that a yes?"

I nodded again, and a tear slipped down my cheek.

He jumped to his feet and placed his big hands on my face.

"Angie... My Angie, don't cry..."

"I'm crying because I'm happy," I choked out. My voice didn't sound particularly sexy right now, but there was nothing I could do about it.

He frowned. "I thought crying meant..."

"No. You can cry when you're happy, just as you can cry when you're sad. I'm happy now. These are tears of happiness." I smiled up at him. Granted, my smile probably didn't look sexy, either. I was a mess. And I needed a shower.

But Thev'rar didn't care. He leaned in and captured my lips in a gentle kiss.

My eyes fluttered close, and I tilted my head and parted my lips to give him access. I wrapped my arms around his neck, and he wrapped his arms around my waist and lifted me. My legs instinctively went to hook around him. He held me like that, ravishing my mouth for a long, blissful minute. When we parted, he looked into my eyes, and I saw so much tenderness there that I knew I was doing the right thing, for once.

"Take me with you. I want to be a princess," I giggled.

"My princess."

"Okay, yours. A life of ease and luxury... that's what you're promising, right?"

He nodded. "You won't have to lift a finger. I'll make sure you have everything."

"That sounds like a better deal than I'd get if I returned to Earth."

"Zorran will be your new home."

We kissed again, and he carried me to his ship. I was grateful, because I didn't think I could walk another step.

He made sure I was comfortable in his cabin, where I could wash and eat, then slip into his bed. As I drifted to sleep, we took off, and I didn't even care enough to get up and take one last look at Sorahan Island. I was glad to have escaped it, and Reazus Prime, at long last.

THEV

We were welcomed with open arms. At the Verde Palace, the guards saluted us, and the advisor to the late king of Zo'kun awaited, with his hands behind his back and a kind smile on his face. When my sister approached him, he bowed deeply. He bowed to me, too, and threw a reluctant glance at Angie. I smiled and nodded, letting him know she was with us.

"Welcome back. My prince. My princess."

"It's good to be back," I said.

"I want to see the king's grave," Ta'sha said. There was pain in her voice, and I immediately felt sorry that she hadn't been there when our father died. I knew she probably felt guilty now. "Will you take me?"

"Of course, my princess."

Ta'sha went with the king's advisor, who would soon become her advisor.

"Oh my God, this is incredible," Angie whispered as she looked around, her bright eyes taking in the mighty forest that surrounded us and the beautiful palace that was built between two giant trees. "Are you sure this is real? Am I dreaming?"

I wrapped my arms around her shoulders and pulled her in. "You're not dreaming," I whispered in her ear. "You're here, with me."

"Oh. My. God."

"You know what? After I show you the palace, I'll take you to the temple, so you can see the Three Heads. You're mentioning your god a lot. I'd love for you to meet mine."

Hand in hand, we walked through the tall doors, and her eyes widened even more when the interior of the Verde Palace revealed itself to us. To me, this was home. I knew every nook and cranny. My sister and I had played hide-and-seek and explored all the rooms and secret tunnels in the walls when we were children. To Angie, it was a whole new world. I loved to see it through her eyes, now. She helped me remember how much I loved my home.

"What are the Three Heads, even? Is it a god with three heads?"

"Yes. Each head has a name, of course, but their names are so sacred, that we're not allowed to utter them. Only the high priest can speak them in his prayers. One head is of a woman, another is of a man, and the third head is of our sacred animal, the kova."

"What is a... kova?"

I led her up the grand staircase and to the second floor, where my chambers were. The corridor was well-lit, and the wall to our right was filled with paintings of the royal family. I stopped in front of one.

"This is my great-great-aunt, and this is a kova." I pointed at the animal next to the beautiful Zokunian woman in her rich dress. She had her hand on the kova's neck.

"But that's a cow!" Angie explained. "It's just a big, green cow!"

I cocked an eyebrow. "So you have kovas on Terra, too?"

"Well, yes. Kind of. Except ours are smaller, not green, and we call them cows. Do your kovas give milk?"

"They do, but their milk is sacred. It is only used in rituals."

"Amazing!"

I smiled. It was a delight to watch her surprise at every little thing she learned. Showing Angie around and teaching her about my world was going to be the greatest time of my life.

"Come. Let me show you my chambers. Let me show you where you'll live. With me."

Her cheeks turned a fascinating shade of pink. I took her hand once more, and she followed me shyly. I didn't understand why she was shy, all of a sudden. On Sorahan Island, that first night we spent on my ship, she hadn't been shy at all. Maybe it was the excitement of all these new discoveries, and the fact that she was in a place that was completely new to her. In a place that was mine, where I was in a position of power, and everyone bowed to me.

My chambers were as I'd left them. The tall windows were wide open, and I could hear the birds chirp in the forest. On the second floor of the palace, I had my own suite of rooms, bathrooms, and even a kitchen, in case I wanted to make something with my own hands. Which I did. Often. Ta'sha was the same. She liked to get her hands dirty from time to time, if only to make a cup of tea. It was one of the reasons we'd both argued a lot with our parents, the king and queen. They had always considered that the royal family should never do anything with their own hands. Except for learning how to wield weapons, in the case of the royal men. When my sister was a little girl, she asked our father to let her learn how to fight, and he'd refused at first. But Ta'sha had always been stubborn, so the king had had to make a compromise. I'd always felt he'd never quite forgiven her for pushing his hand back then. And since then, their relationship had suffered, and only our mother could keep the peace.

It was all in the past now. Our parents were gone. The kingdom was ours, and our duty was to rule it with devotion and fairness. Ta'sha was going to be queen, and now that I wasn't going to become a priest anymore, I would be by her side.

"But this is... this is more than I imagined," Angie said, snapping me out of my trance. She let go of my hand and carefully stepped forward, turning in place, her eyes taking everything in. "This is all yours?"

"Ours."

"Good God! Or good... umm... Three Heads!"

I laughed.

"This is too much space. I'll get lost."

"In our chambers?" I laughed harder. "I doubt it. But in the palace? For sure."

I walked into the grand bath and was satisfied to see that a servant had already filled the tub with warm, scented water. I started removing my weapons and my clothes. I heard Angie chuckle behind me, and when I turned to her, I saw her face was all pink and she was looking at me with a mischievous sparkle in her eyes.

"Come take a bath with me."

"A bath?! That's a whole pool!"

Indeed, the tub was large, and placed under a tall window that was open and offered a view of the mountains in the distance. But it was not a pool. It was a royal tub, fit for a prince, and now, a princess.

I extended my hand, and she took it. I was naked before her, and she was trying her hardest not to blatantly stare at me. Too bad. Because I liked it when she stared at me.

"May I?"

She nodded, and I started removing her clothes. We'd both washed on the ship, not wanting to make our appearance at the court in the state we were in after the adventures on the island. But it had been quick and unsatisfactory. We needed a long, relaxing bath.

I unwrapped her like a gift, tracing my fingers over her soft skin. She wasn't as pale as when I'd first met her. The two suns of Reazus Prime had given her skin a warm, glowing tan. I removed her shirt, and then her trousers and boots. She was now standing before me in the two contraptions that I'd seen before and still didn't understand. She called the first one a bra, and the second one – undies. They were new to me, as no male or female in Zo'kun wore such things. But of course, our females didn't own the round, full heavy breasts that my Angie owned.

I was fascinated with them. The second she removed the bra herself, my hands were on them. I felt the nipples harden under my touch. My cock throbbed and grew in size, which caused Angie to giggle and take a step back.

I frowned.

"Sorry. You just... Well, you poked me."

I frowned again. For someone who'd convinced me to touch her when I was certain I wanted to become a priest, she was awfully embarrassed now, when we were naked, and we belonged to each other.

I pulled her back against me, and my cock rested on her soft belly. She trembled.

"My beautiful mate." I kissed her lips gently. "We'll spend a lot of time like this. Just the two of us, naked, embraced. I want to be inside you all day and all night. And I know I'll not tire of you."

She bit her lip and looked up into my eyes. "All day and all night? That's... bold." Then her gaze drifted between us. She wrapped a hand around my cock. "I'm not sure you'll fit in the first place... Then to have you inside me for that long... I don't know. You might break me in two."

"Your body will get used to me. You will crave me, as I crave you."

"That..." She swallowed hard. I could smell her arousal. "I wouldn't mind that happening."

I bent down and rolled the undies down her legs. My fingers brushed her mound, and I heard her breathe in sharply. I grinned and started exploring, pushing my fingers between her soft folds that were covered in light hair. She moaned and dug her nails into my shoulders. I pressed my nose to her mound and inhaled deeply. My mouth watered at the scent of her. I'd twanted to taste her for so long, and now I finally had my chance. I knew that if I had one taste, I would become addicted.

"Oh, Thev..."

She trembled as I pushed my tongue between her folds and lapped at her juices. Their sweetness went straight to my brain, like a drug, and I pushed her thighs apart, hooking one of her legs around my shoulder. She was now holding onto my head and my back, guiding me where she needed me most.

I licked from the sweet entrance of her pussy, up to her clitoris. Her female parts were smaller and more sensitive than the parts of any female of my species. I noticed that she squirmed and moaned at every gesture that I made. It was easy to pleasure her, to make her come, when she was so beautifully responsive. Her moans and whimpers were music to my ears. I wanted to give her orgasm after orgasm, just to hear her sing.

I circled her clit with the tip of my tongue, and she hooked her fingers into my hair.

"More... oh... please, don't stop..."

As if I'd ever stop. Didn't she know that by now?

I licked her faster while pushing one finger into her soaked pussy. Her walls throbbed with need, squeezed me and pulled my finger in, desperate for more. I moved it in and out, and the more I fucked her like that, the wetter she grew. I moved my tongue up and down her slit, eager to drink every drop of juice, and when she grunted in frustration, I went back to teasing her clit until her thighs tensed and she let out a little scream.

She held on to me tightly as she rode the first orgasm, and I was just happy to lick her lazily, clean her thoroughly before I made her come again. I pushed a second finger inside her pussy, stretching her and preparing her for what was next.

"Oh, Thev... This is too much. I need to... I need to sit down."

I chuckled and rose to my feet. I took her hand and guided her to the tub, then helped her in. She hadn't lied. Her knees were wobbly, and she needed to rest before I could take her, truly take her, and make her my mate. My cock was painfully hard, and when we were finally in the water, she tried to wrap her hands around it, but I stopped her. I didn't want her hands. I didn't even want her mouth. All I wanted was her pussy.

I washed her gently for a few minutes and allowed her to recover, then I pulled her onto my lap. She wrapped her legs around me and lifted her hips. All the while, she held my gaze and smiled at me. She looked like the happiest, most fulfilled woman in the world, and I was glad I was the one who made her feel that way.

And this was only the beginning.

ANGIE

The water was warm, and it smelled amazing. There were scented oils in it, and petals floated on the surface. The light poured through the wide-open windows, and the song of the exotic birds filled the air. This was luxury like I'd never seen before.

Thev's lips traveled from my jaw to my neck. As I knelt on top of him, straddling his hips, I felt the tip of his cock tease my entrance. He had one hand around the base, and he was guiding it gently, up and down my slit, until he mercifully pushed it in an inch, just enough to ignite my imagination further.

His mouth found my breast, and then my nipple. He sucked lightly, sending shivers right down to my core. I closed my eyes and moaned. I wanted to enjoy every minute of this. There was no point in rushing, when I knew this was going to be the rest of my life.

He worked my nipple until it was painfully hard, then moved to the other. He worshiped my big, heavy breasts like no other man had done before. He worshiped all my body the same, every roll and stretch mark. Things other men had been bothered by... he was delighted by them! I had never felt so beautiful. And the fact that we were making love in the middle of the day, in all this natural light... It was new to me. It might've been scary, had he not shown such genuine passion for every part of my body that was not flat and fit.

When we'd arrived, I'd seen the Zokunian women. They all looked like Ta'sha – tall, lean, strong, muscular. They had narrow hips and small breasts. I would've expected a Zokunian man to be attracted to that and that alone. Maybe most of them were. I was just lucky Thev was different.

He was even different for a prince. He was capable, he knew how to fight, and he could provide for himself and others. The fact that he'd gone looking for his sister without taking his guards and a bunch of servants with him spoke volumes of the type of man he was.

"Angie, you're so soft... so sexy..."

His words brought me back to the present. His hand went to my hips, where he kneaded my flesh as he pushed another inch of his cock inside me. I opened my eyes and looked at him.

"You like that? That I'm... soft?"

"Yes. I like everything about you. Your body... is perfect."

My heart wanted to jump out of my chest and hug him. That was impossible and silly, so I hugged him instead.

He grunted as he hid his head between my breasts and slipped his cock in all the way.

I gasped, taken by surprise. He was big, but he'd prepared me enough that I didn't feel much pain. Just a slight burn that was quickly replaced by pure pleasure when he started bouncing me on top of him. Both his hands were on my hips now, and he lifted me easily, then impaled me onto his cock. I grabbed the edges of the tub and started moving, too, determined to not let him do all the work.

Looking into his eyes, it hit me that this was the first time when I was on top. No one had let me ride them before. Not only was Thev not stressed about it, but he enjoyed looking at me as we increased the pace and my breasts bounced freely. He took in everything, his eyes filled with love and lust.

I could feel tension building in my core. The water splashed around us, and my moans turned louder and louder. I was close... so close... And it hadn't even taken long. The way his cock felt inside me... He was long, and thick, and every time the tip pressed against my cervix, I murmured Thev's name and increased the pace. I was bouncing so fast that my legs were starting to ache. But I couldn't stop. I needed this... I needed him...

"Angie..."

"Shh... shut up... fuck me... just... shut up and fuck me."

He grinned and pushed his hips up to meet me. His cock was rubbing places inside me that I hadn't even known existed. The tension built until it was too much, and I threw my head back and screamed as I came hard. I felt myself gush, and I let go, allowing the powerful orgasm to take over my body.

All thoughts flew out of my mind, and I was just here, in this moment, with Thev, his cock deep inside me, my pussy throbbing, my body shaking with the intensity of my release.

When I came down from it somewhat, I realized Thev hadn't come. I looked at him, confused. But before I could say anything, he flipped us over, turned me around, and pressed me against the edge of the tub. My back was to him, and I felt his cock slip back inside me. This time, my pussy welcomed him eagerly, wet and stretched, ready for more.

I held on as he rammed me from behind. He wasn't gentle this time, and I didn't want him to be. One of his hands came to squeeze my breast, and I thrust back to meet him every time, until I was too exhausted, and I couldn't move anymore. He fucked me so fast and so hard that I couldn't keep up with him. I relinquished control. He growled and grunted, and started kissing and biting my neck. Every nip made me shudder. I could feel his tusks, and I couldn't believe how much they turned me on.

"Angie... I can't... I have to..."

"Come inside me," I moaned. "I want to feel you come inside me."

"Yes. I'll fill you with my seed."

That brought me closer and closer to my own release. If I had a third orgasm today, I thought I would just faint.

"I'll fill you and put a baby in you," he continued.

And that did it. I came with a scream, my pussy throbbing and squeezing him, and this time, he came too, with a deep, wild grunt. I felt his cock grow bigger and shoot stream after stream of hot cum at the entrance of my womb. We stayed like that for minutes on end, him emptying every drop he had to give, until I felt some of his cum seep out and into the water. I was so full, and when he pulled out, it rushed out of me. He turned me around and kissed me fiercely.

"Well, I think we're done with our bath," I said, giggling.

He chuckled. "But I'm not done with you."

We got out, and he wrapped me in a big, fluffy towel, and then took me in his arms and carried me to the bedroom. We found the table filled with plates of fruit. It was alien fruit to me, but I saw things that looked like mangoes, peaches, and even grapes. He set me onto the bed, and as I threw the towel off and snuggled under the duvet naked, he brought a plate.

"What is this?"

"Taste."

He slipped a grape into my mouth, and I found out it wasn't a grape at all. The taste was sweet and aromatic, reminding me of strawberries. Not, it was more than that. More complex. It was like strawberry jam mixed with roses.

"This is amazing," I said as I chewed.

"These are wild, foraged in the forest. That's why they're so tasty."

"More, please."

For the next hour, he fed me fruit, and we talked about nothing in particular. We simply enjoyed each other's presence and lazed around, not having a care in the world.

I could get used to this life.

"See, this is why I didn't want to become king," he said later. "Too many responsibilities, too much work... My sister is going to regret her position soon." He laughed. "Not really, but you know what I mean. She'll be a great queen."

"It suits me just fine. Being mated to a prince is good enough."

"I hope it is." He kissed my shoulder. "I will take care of you, Angelica. I love you."

My heart fluttered. I looked into his eyes. "I love you, too."

We kissed, and I couldn't quite wrap my mind around the fact that... here I was, after having been abducted by aliens, in this bed, in a royal palace, on an alien planet.

I was never going to return home. My family and my friends would think something bad had happened to me, and they would look for me until they'd give up. That made me feel a little sad, so I made a mental note to ask Thev'rar in the following days if he might allow me to visit my family at least once and let them know that I was okay. I could tell them that I'd decided to move to Bali. Maybe I could find a way to send them a letter from time to time, without giving away the fact that I wasn't on Earth anymore.

I was sure Thev would figure something out if I asked him.

But for now... For now, I was going to enjoy this, because I deserved it. I'd gone through enough, and for sure, it beat the job at the bank. And even visiting the pyramids.

"I love you," he whispered again in my ear, then pushed me onto my back and climbed on top of me.

I traced his copper tattoos as he entered me again, and when he leaned in, instead of kissing him, I stuck out my tongue and licked one of his tusks. He growled and sank his hand in my hair. Holding me like that, he fucked me fast and hard, until I screamed his name.

"Mine. You're mine. Say it."

"I'm yours."

And I wouldn't have it any other way.

ANGIE

I woke up to the flutter of wings over my head. I opened my eyes and smiled at the colorful bird that pecked at Thev's pillow. A month had passed since I came to the palace, and I wasn't yet bored of this morning routine.

Thev woke up early and went about his royal duties. His sister, the queen, needed him often, and he tried to see her before I woke up, so he could then spend more time with me.

And me... well, I loved to sleep in.

I sat up, and the bird looked at me curiously, then flew back out the window. Breakfast was waiting on the table in the next room. I lazily got out of the bed and padded there to fill a cup of tea and take it to the window, where I loved to sit and just meditate for a few minutes. There was no rush. There was nothing that I needed to do, so no need to even think about the day ahead. I simply enjoyed my tea and soaked up the sun.

Then, I went to wash myself and brush my hair, so I could slip into a comfortable dress. I sat down and started having my breakfast when Thev walked in.

"Good morning, beautiful!"

"Good morning."

He walked over and kissed me on the cheek, then sat down, and I poured him a cup of tea.

"How is our queen today?"

"Stressed because of the festivities. She wants everything to be perfect."

The day of the Three Heads was coming, and the whole kingdom was equally excited and agitated. It was a sacred day, when the statue was taken out of the temple and carried through the capital. Zokunians from all over had already flooded the city in the forest, and there was a constant hustle and bustle. I loved it, but on the other hand... I wasn't involved in any way, so I could just sit back and enjoy what was happening. No one ever asked me to do anything. Every time I offered, Thev reminded me that I was his royal mate, and as a royal mate, I didn't have to lift a finger.

That suited me just fine. I spent my days reading – the palace had a huge library that occupied an entire tower. I often retreated there and forgot to eat or sleep. I'd also taken up painting, and the queen herself had once praised my skills. It meant a lot coming from her. Her personal collection was hosted in the other tower of the palace, and few people were allowed in there.

"The festivities are going to be perfect, I'm sure."

"They will," he said. "This is your first time attending, and I want the day of the Three Heads to make an impression."

I giggled. They kind of hoped that he might convert me one day. He'd never said it, but I suspected it. It didn't bother me, really. I'd never been religious, even though he thought I was by the frequency with which I mentioned God. It had been impossible to convince him that they were just expressions.

"I wanted to ask you," he started, a bit hesitantly.

"What?" I spread jam on a piece of bread. Yes, the Zokunians had bread, and I was eternally grateful.

"Would you like... I mean... Would you consider riding the sacred kova through the city?"

"What?!" I dropped the knife and stared at him. "Ride a cow through the city?"

"Yes." He'd gotten used to my calling the kovas they worshiped so much green cows. Because that was what they were. No offense. "It's tradition. A lady of the court would ride the sacred kova on the first day of the festivities. I would like it to be you."

"Maybe Ta'sha would like..."

He shook his head. "Ta'sha did it before she was queen. Many times. She can't do it now. It has to be a lady of the court, not the queen."

"Ride a cow..." I bit the inside of my lip, looking at him reluctantly. "I don't know."

The kovas were huge. I called them cows, but in truth, they were the bigger, taller, wider cousins of cows. They were kind, tender creatures, and they were allowed to roam freely through the forest. They weren't dangerous.

"I would be honored if you said yes," he insisted.

"And I'm honored that you asked... I just wonder... Wouldn't your people disagree with it? I'm not one of you."

At that, he straightened his back and puffed up his chest. "You are my mate."

"Well, yes. But I'm still not one of you. I don't look like you, I don't worship the Three Heads... I don't want the Zokunians to think I'm an intruder, or that I'm disrespecting the... I don't know... your culture, your traditions."

"No one will think that!" He took my hands in his and looked deep into my eyes. "You are my mate, Angie, and it doesn't matter that your skin is not green, that your teeth are blunt, and your hair is yellow."

I laughed. "My teeth are blunt... Yeah, that's the problem!"

"Please say yes. You will ride the sacred kova in a sheer, golden dress, and you will be the most beautiful woman the kingdom has ever seen."

I blushed. "Well, when you put it like that... Then, yes. I'll do it."

"Thank you!" He kissed me passionately, and I relaxed in his arms. "I love you," he whispered against my lips.

"I love you too, even when you put me in these complicated situations."

"There's nothing complicated about it. You just have to... go out there and be your beautiful self."

"I think I can do that."

We finished our breakfast, and I retreated to the library, while Thev went to give the queen the good news.

On my way to the tower, I passed by one of the big, green cows that liked to graze in the palace gardens. I approached it slowly, and she raised her head to greet me. She tilted her head, and I scratched her behind the ear.

"Kova," I whispered. "I might as well call you by your sacred name."

The animal mooed, and that made it even harder for me to not think of it as just a green cow. I laughed and patted her on the back.

Later, as I finally climbed the spiral staircase up to the library, I stopped to gaze through one of the small windows. I could see the forest that surrounded us, and the houses of the Zokunians neatly tucked between the trees. The trees were huge here, their crowns aiming for the sky. The city was built in perfect harmony with the forest. In the distance, I could see the mountains.

This was my home.

Thev'rar was my home.

I was the luckiest girl alive.

THE END

Outlaw Planet Mates

Alien's Mercy, by Leslie Chase

Alien's Treasure, by Elin Wyn

Alien's Challenge, by Nancey Cummings

Alien's Stone Heart, by Lynnea Lee

Alien's Fate, by Eden Ember

Aliens' Sacrifice, by Cady Austin

Alien's Jewel, by Ava York

Alien's Wild Mate, by Sonia Nova

Alien's Fire, by Lynnea Lee

Alien's Power, by Eden Ember

Aliens' Princess, by Cady Austin

More sci-fi romance by Cara Wylde

Monster Hearts
Heart of an Orc
Heart of a Naga
Heart of a Kraken
Heart of a Minotaur
Heart of a Gargoyle

About the Author

Cara Wylde loves to write about strong, feisty women and their hot Alphas who will do anything to make them happy. Her books are filled with romance and just a dash of mystery, suspense, and that eerie atmosphere she fell in love with reading too many gothic novels.

When she's not writing, Cara is reading, planning her next story, or daydreaming.

Subscribe to Cara Wylde's Newsletter
Scan the QR code